Alpha Wave

To,
Patti and Jason
two great neighbors
and friends. Let
me know what you
think!
Julie

Julie Parsons

To order additional copies of this book, contact:
Xlibris Corporation
1-888-795-4274
www.Xlibris.com
Orders@Xlibris.com
100378

To everyone that encouraged me to write, even when it drove me crazy.
You know who you are.

Ally

How did everything get so messed up?

Sleeping in the back of my Chevy Impala was not my idea of living the good life. In fact, I couldn't remember the last time that I could truly convince myself that my life was on track. The only thing that had been going in my favor was college.

Of course, no matter how well I did on essays, exams, and generously offered extra credit (which ends after freshman year by the way), there was still the matter of handing over a huge hunk of cash. The dean sent a letter and offered congratulations on making his list.

Great, but what about the fact that I couldn't afford to stay in school? Scholarships? Yeah, right, educational funding was the first to go when the economy started getting sucked down the crapper.

I couldn't say that no one would help me. I wasn't the best person at asking for help. I couldn't even confront my own family about finances, and because of that less-than-ideal character trait, I avoided my parents when I knew I couldn't afford another semester at Central Michigan University. Instead I did what everyone else in my family did best—I found a way to ignore my problems and dig myself deeper in the hole.

By the time the second semester of sophomore year rolled around, I had a 3.9 GPA and was dropping out of college. Unsurprisingly, my mother was furious. Still, I felt that no one could top the anger that I felt. I couldn't help but point out that it was not completely my fault that I could not afford college seeing as a part-time job as a cashier wouldn't pay a $12,000 yearly tuition.

I thought about a story I had heard in which a girl confessed to her mother that she was pregnant and moving in with her boyfriend. The mother had completely flipped out, crying hysterically on the kitchen floor until the girl finally reassured her mother that she was not pregnant after all and that she had *only* flunked out of two of her classes.

Predictably, I told my mother the straight-up truth that I couldn't afford to stay in college and was promptly informed that I would be either packing my bags or paying a monthly rent to stay. What can I say? My anger got the best of me. By the time I made it to Indiana, I had a quarter tank of gas, twenty dollars in cash, and an increasing sense of overwhelming anxiety coupled with exhaustion.

I didn't want to go to a motel. Hell, I probably couldn't afford a motel at that point, but I was getting more and more tired as each white line blurred past. I finally decided to pull over to the side of the road and sleep in the back of the car. I had a bunch of blankets in my trunk, and the weather was only just starting to get colder, so I figured I could last the night in my car and then try to come up with a better plan when I was well rested and a little less emotional.

I came to a stop, making sure that I was far enough from the side of the road so I wouldn't have to waste the battery on hazard lights. I popped the trunk open and climbed out the passenger side door, still paranoid that a speeding car would barrel down the road, taking my door and my arm with it. I kept my head down as I walked to the back of my car, trying to keep the brisk autumn air off my face.

My trunk creaked open as I gave it the customary pounding required to make it cooperate. Don't get me wrong, my car was practically pristine thanks to many hours of work put in by my father and myself, but for some reason we never could get rid of that trunk's stubborn streak. I grabbed the blankets and then hunkered in for the night in the backseat of the car. I used the armrest as a pillow, and while my resting place of choice lacked the comfort of a five-star hotel, I still had no trouble dozing off as I recounted the past weeks of bickering with my mother. At least she wouldn't wake me up in a few hours, demanding to hear the plans I made for my life. Honestly, I was completely lost in the subject area of planning for my future. I couldn't see where I would be even a month from then.

Ally

As I slept, I dreamed that I was falling, the dream that everyone has had at least once. I expected to wake up seconds before I hit the ground but suddenly found myself at the bottom of a huge, cavernous hole that smelled like wet, moldy wood. If emotion could fill space, I would swear that despair flooded the hole to the top. The walls were almost translucent, more like moving shadows than physical matter, and I lost myself as I stared into their swirling depths.

I felt a pair of eyes fixed on the back of my head. Too afraid to look, but unable to ignore the feeling, I contemplated my plan of action. I'd seen too many horror movies, and my instincts weren't to wait around and be killed. That being said, I knew that investigation of the creepy, make-your-guts-twist-and-turn-in-your-stomach surroundings often lead to a slow miserable death as well. Still, I slowly and carefully turned around, discovering that more than one person was watching me.

"Hello?" I said, more of a question than a greeting. At the best of times, I had a difficult time talking to other people, which wasn't a trait that improved when they were all staring at me like zombies. They continued to watch me as if they were waiting for me to do something.

I fidgeted nervously, noticing how awkwardly I held myself as the three people continued to stare.

There was an older man in the middle with salt-and-pepper hair and dark brown eyes. His eyes pulled me into their depths, almost as bottomless and full of despair as the well. I began wondering whether or not he was really as old as he looked or if it was just the expression planted on his pale, weathered face. Watching the skin around his eyes wrinkle, I would almost think that he was just concentrating on a difficult problem. But the sadness in his eyes—eyes that told me to run away and come closer at the same time—told me that there was no simple solution to his problem.

Next to him stood a petite woman with slate gray eyes and blonde hair also staring at me, trying to master the art of killing me with her eyes. Even on my mother's worst days, it never looked like she was about to murder me. I couldn't understand why she was so angry with me.

But another face pulled me away from her black hole of rage before I began to wake up. He looked so scared that I couldn't help but wonder if I wasn't supposed to be there. But what could pity, hate, and fear have in common toward the one action of me falling into their space? Whatever they meant, I couldn't interpret their possible reasons with my haze-filled brain.

I snapped awake jumping up with a shriek and bumping my head on the roof of my car.

"Crap!" I shouted at the empty car, holding my hands to my head. I noticed that it was still dark outside as I nursed my bruised skull and tried to stop shaking.

I fished my phone out of my pocket, hoping that the battery wasn't dead just yet. The screen on my phone told me that it was about three-thirty-three in the morning, which was odd because I had passed out only an hour earlier. Usually when I slept during the school semester, and even during the summer, I was out for a solid seven hours, maybe more if I stayed up late studying or watching television.

The time was the least of my worries, but analyzing my sleep schedule was the only thing I could do at that moment to keep myself preoccupied. Even when I was little, I couldn't handle nightmares. They always left me unsettled, afraid that if I closed my eyes I would find myself right back in the dreamscape. Or maybe if I closed my eyes, the scary man chasing me in my dream would open my closet door and creep toward me quietly with an ominous-looking butcher knife the minute I let my guard down.

Despite feeling shaken up, I didn't completely register that the feeling of being watched was still very much present. It was only after I let myself relax again that I realized the anxiety was not entirely because of my nightmare. I swept my eyes over my surroundings wondering if perhaps someone really was watching me.

I guess a person that watches too many horror movies even though they leave her with nightmares and an overactive imagination shouldn't run away from home in the middle of the night. As my gaze turned from behind me to the side of the road, I noticed an old, decrepit barn that looked as though a gust of wind would cause the walls to collapse. In fact, a few boards had fallen from the side of the building, and a section of the roof had begun to sag, doing its best to fight against gravity. The whole scene reminded me of a haunted house I had visited a few Halloweens ago.

Leave it to me to find the most deserted, disturbing place to stop my car.

I obviously wasn't going to go out there in the middle of the night to investigate. That would fall under the "just plain stupid" category. On the other hand, I couldn't sink back into a restful sleep after noticing the eerie old shack, so the only solution was to get back on the road even if I had no idea of my exact destination.

As I climbed back into the driver's seat, I heard a scream that would make even the toughest marine's hair stand on end. I had never heard anyone scream like that, whether from pain or fear I couldn't tell. Indecision plagued me once again.

If Freddie Krueger—another villain of a horror movie that I shouldn't have watched—was out there, I was not going to interfere. I mean, I didn't believe in running away when someone needed help, but Freddie killed everyone. I wasn't even sure what happened at the end of that movie, but someone that could control dreams like Freddie wouldn't be stopped by a scared nineteen-year-old.

Well, instead of running away like I wanted to, I smacked myself on the forehead (completely forgetting that I had just bumped it a few minutes ago) and forced myself to remain rational. Freddie Krueger was not real, and no matter how badly I had screwed up over the last few months, I wasn't going to turn my back on someone in need.

I took a deep breath, opened the car door, and stepped outside. Naturally, the screaming resonated again, from nowhere other than the ominous barn, making me do a double take and almost trip over myself as I tried to get a grip. What was someone doing out there in the middle of the night?

Ha, kind of like you? I thought to myself. I reached for my cell phone to call 911, not believing I didn't think of that before I went through the whole Freddie debate.

I also couldn't believe that I had almost wandered into that creepy old shack all by myself when I had a means of contacting help, especially after watching all those ditsy horror movie girls run around screaming hopelessly, cell phone within reach the whole time. Of course, it wouldn't have been in their pocket because in most of those movies they're wearing a tight tank top and underwear. Honestly, how many girls really do that?

As I opened my phone, I saw that there were no bars. Okay, so I couldn't contact help but I could at least walk in that door as prepared as possible. The only defensive weapon I could find was the Maglite flashlight Dad always forced me to keep in my car.

"*Hold it over your head like this so you can hit 'em in the head,*" he would say as he demonstrated proper skull-crushing technique.

With flashlight in hand, I began slowly walking toward the building, trying to make as little sound as possible with each step I took. The screaming had stopped, and I couldn't hear anyone else, making me wonder if maybe the girl was alone in the building. Maybe my silly worries had made me too late. Holding my breath, resolving not to be a complete pansy, I walked into the barn and gasped at the scene before me.

From the outside, the barn looked like a glorified, oversized outhouse, but the main room was at least forty feet high. I rubbed my eyes and pinched myself thinking that I must have still been dreaming in the backseat of my Impala.

Two sprawling staircases made out of what looked like marble met in the middle right in front of me. A crystal chandelier hung over the point where the stairs met. I really must have smacked my head harder than I thought. I began to walk around and explore the intricate pattern that the polished black and white floor tiles made. In the center, underneath the chandelier and between the staircases, there was a beautiful marble sun with a yin-yang in the center.

However, the yin-yang did not consist of the typical black and white coloring. Instead, the black and white morphed into different shades of gray toward the middle of the circle. I walked toward it slowly, noticing how my position in relation to the sun changed the way it looked. As I got closer, it almost seemed to burn more and more brightly.

"Stop!" a male voice yelled from above. I froze in place and quickly glanced up to the top of the staircase.

"Oh," was my completely unintelligible response to the older man that looked unsettlingly like the man in my dream. My eyes darted quickly to the blood spattered over his chest right before I passed out.

Ally

"Do you think we should tell her?"

"Of course we should. Are you an idiot or something?"

"No, but maybe we should just wait. This can be a lot to handle."

"Really? You don't say!"

"Okay, there's no reason to be facetious."

"Well, if you wouldn't have been so careless, I wouldn't have gotten slaughtered yet again!"

"Ha? Careless? It was your fault."

"So I got a little angry."

"A little angry? You were trying to kill me! Besides this has nothing to do with her."

"Fine, don't tell her. Just let her fall into a trap and die. That should send a pretty clear message."

"Both of you need to stop. What's done is done. This isn't something that someone should have to wake up to in the middle of. If and when we tell her, we need to be tactful about it."

It took me a while to wake up again. Maybe I was finally getting my seven hours. I remembered people arguing, but I couldn't tell if I was dreaming

14

or awake. I hated when I woke up and couldn't remember whether I did something or if it was just a dream. My dreams always seemed so real that I could still feel them when I woke up.

One time someone stabbed me right in the stomach during one of my dreams. When I woke up, my stomach hurt more than I thought possible for an unreal injury. Even after a few minutes, there was still a little bit of a tingle. It couldn't possibly have been real though; some girl had said something about getting slaughtered.

"Good morning," a cheery voice exclaimed from the corner of the room, making me jump halfway out of bed. As I crouched behind the side of the bed, I caught sight of the man from the stairs and felt a cold stab of fear. He looked relaxed, if not tired, in an overstuffed armchair. Had he killed that screaming girl? Still, something in his eyes told me no. He reminded me of the older man from my dream. He had the same sadness in his eyes.

"Sorry for scaring you. My name is John, and I just thought you might like to wake up with someone here for you," he explained.

"Where am I?" I asked, half expecting him to manically tell me his twisted story with me playing the part of his captive.

I looked around, finding the door first. The door was to my right, and next to it stood a huge wardrobe made of cherrywood. Knowing where my exit was, I began to look around, keeping the man in my peripheral vision.

I had been in a king-sized bed with a deep burgundy-colored comforter. The bedposts, also made out of cherrywood, were carved into hundreds of beautiful swirls that I could have stared at for hours. Across the room from me, I caught sight of my reflection in a mirror that covered half the wall. I needed a shower and a brush. I doubted that anything less than a half bottle of conditioner wouldn't be able to get those tangles out.

"You remember walking into the building?" the man asked suddenly, bringing me back to the present.

"Yes, of course. You mean the barn?" I asked, not believing that anyone could refer to the place that I walked into as a building

"Well . . . the structure of the building looks different to different people," he told me slowly.

"Okay, well, as much as I'd like to debate you on that point, if you could just tell me you're not some kind of pedophile or something, that would be great. I saw blood on your shirt," I accused, wondering whether accusation was a bad idea. Maybe if I played dumb instead he would leave me alone for a while longer.

He laughed, his face transforming within seconds. He went from looking at least sixty to looking like a man in his fifties or maybe even forties.

"I was making spaghetti. Damn good spaghetti too, but unfortunately I ended up wearing it instead of eating it. I'm not going to hurt you," he added suddenly.

Still, there was something in his voice that left me with a shred of doubt. The way he said *"I'm not going to hurt you"* reminded me of my best friend, Shelly. She would always tell part lie and part truth because she thought that she would be more likely to get away with lying. Unfortunately, she was such a terrible liar that even that wasn't enough. She couldn't lie to save her life.

I shifted my attention away from my internal babbling and back to the man. Had he done something to another girl? Why would he do something to her and not to me? Even though I didn't think he had killed the girl, my first impression of people was rarely ever right. I started to panic, sifting through all of the half-learned defensive moves I had picked up from my friends that took karate.

Of course in the end the defensive moves that stuck out the most were the ones I had seen Sandra Bullock perform in *Miss Congeniality*. If worse came to worst, a punch to the groin would have to do.

"Where's the girl that was screaming?" I asked slowly, keeping my eyes on his face and measuring every movement. I was getting ready to make a run for it when something on his face made me stop. He seemed almost apologetic.

"I know you have a lot of questions. I have a lot of answers, but you wouldn't even consider asking the questions for most of them. I'm not trying to keep anything from you, but this . . . this situation can be a lot to handle."

"Okay, just start from the beginning," I demanded, crossing my arms like a stubborn toddler.

"When people enter this . . . house, they can't leave," he told me, not entering story mode as I had expected.

"What do you mean they can't leave?" My heart accelerated, pushing me to consider flight over fight.

"Hold on now. Don't freak out on me. *I'm* not holding you captive, I promise."

"Well then, if you're not, who is? Is there someone else?" I squeaked, wondering whether or not I should have my back toward the door.

"Unfortunately there's no one else. We have no idea why we can't leave." He stared at his hands.

"Don't tell me the *house* won't let us leave." I rolled my eyes at that ridiculous notion. If I wanted to leave, I could have just found those amazing stairs, walked out the door, got in my car, and left that insane situation behind. Pitifully, the house was looking a lot more enticing than any other option I had at the moment.

"When you hear the rest of the story, a house that won't let anyone leave will seem normal."

"Okay, go on," I encouraged.

"Whatever won't let us leave also won't let us die." He stared down at his hands.

"That's ridiculous." Okay, the guy was seriously delusional. Or maybe someone was just playing some sick practical joke on me. Maybe Ashton Kutcher was snickering in some studio as his crew recorded me being duped for *Punk'd*. The only problem was that I wasn't a celebrity. No one cared about me.

"Okay, so let's say you fell down the stairs and broke your neck. Are you just going to walk around with your neck bent to the side?" I challenged.

"Well, we do die . . . but then we come back." He watched me as if he thought I was about to have an emotional breakdown. If anyone was going to have a breakdown, it would be him. I should've just stayed in my car.

"So the girl that I heard screaming?" I asked, trying to direct him back to one of my major concerns.

"That would be Jane," he explained, grimacing.

"And she *died*?" I stood up, reasoning that I would get a better jump start to the door.

"Yes, but now she's back," he reassured me, eyes registering my every action.

"Okay, prove it. Prove that she's still alive," I demanded.

"Alive again, you mean." He sounded almost like he had given up on convincing me of the situation.

"Sure, whatever. Although you're going to have a pretty hard time proving that she died in the first place."

"All right, I'll be back in a few minutes. Please just promise me you won't start wandering around. You see, this house can be quite dangerous to the untrained eye," he warned.

"Is that a threat?" I was suddenly afraid just to step out of the room. I thought about all the traps that the crazy serial killer set in the house in the *Saw II* movie. I thought of guns pointed at doors and pits full of needles. My throat began to close off as I imagined that even then noxious gas was filling the room.

"Of course not. Believe me, when you learn all the perils in this house, you'll laugh at the fact that, of all things, *I* scared you."

His words caused a shiver to run down my spine as he left the room. Even if I had been thinking about running away or exploring, my feet were suddenly firmly planted on the floor.

Ally

I kept myself at arm's length as John left the room. He closed the door quickly, only looking back at me briefly. I heard laughter in the hallway and rushed to the door, planting my ear on the wooden panel.

"This is too fast," another male voice argued. "We're supposed to let them get used to the surroundings, not force everything on them in less than an hour."

"Well, we're kind of running out of time," a female voice spat venomously.

"I already told her, so this argument is useless," John cut in.

"She wants to see you, Jane," he added, his voice getting closer to the door.

I jumped back and sat on the bed. I tried to look at ease, but my hands were folded over my lap, and my body kept shifting awkwardly as I tried to keep my back to the wall.

John came back maybe seconds later with a grumpy-looking girl following behind. She was quite short, shorter than my five-foot-four stature. She must've only barely broken the five-foot line. She had blonde hair and cold gray eyes. That frown was going to cause serious wrinkles somewhere down the line. When the girl caught sight of me, her grumpiness turned to outrage.

"What do you want?" she demanded. Her eyes raked over me. She was assessing me, and it appeared that she was not satisfied with what she saw.

"She says she heard you screaming," John explained.

"Oh, for the love of God!" Grumpy shouted.

"This is Jane," John explained. "She was the one you heard screaming."

"Were you really the one screaming? Are you okay?" I asked, thinking that Grumpy would prove as a very fitting nickname. I could already tell the girl rarely ever experienced happiness. The frown seemed to be permanently glued on her face.

"Yes and yes. I'm fine, so can I go now?" Jane directed her last comment toward John, completely ignoring me. She stood there with her arms crossed until John answered.

"Of course," John said. "Right after you tell her why you were screaming."

"And who are *you*?" Jane sneered at me.

"I-I'm Ally," I stammered, barely daring to look her in the eye.

"Well, *Ally*, I was screaming because of this idiot named David. Because of him, I fell into the center of that *cool* looking sun in between the stairs in the main room. Go ahead and try it sometime, it's a blast." She eyed me speculatively, looking clearly disappointed.

"Jane! Don't be cruel," John chastised. "Ally, you shouldn't go anywhere near that sun. Anyone who steps inside of the circle is burned to death."

"You seriously want me to believe that you guys have died and come back?" I asked, completely fed up with the whole situation. I would be more likely to believe that Freddie Krueger existed at that point.

"Well, I guess you'll just have to see it for yourself sometime. Maybe it'll even be you that dies," Jane supplied happily. The girl was starting to give me the psycho vibe.

"All right," John interrupted. "Now that you know I haven't killed anyone, I would like to show you around and introduce you to the rest of the people living here."

"You haven't proven anything yet," I prompted. "If anything, you've shown me that she's just as crazy as you are."

"Okay, well, allow me to introduce you to the rest of the crazies then."

David

I referred to the doctor as John when I was angry. I didn't speak to him at all when I was outraged. But at that moment, I didn't even know if I wanted to be in the same room with him. Well, I did want to be in the same room with him because he was still in there with the girl, and she had just woken up. But he had kicked Jane and me out, and he was letting Jane back in without me.

Introducing her to Jane first was like sending a homeless looking man to close a business deal. There was no way Jane was the right person to welcome a stranger into the house. I paced back and forth in front of the door waiting for some sign that I could enter or that Jane would leave soon.

After a few minutes, Jane left the room looking perturbed and anxious to get away from the new girl.

"Not pretty enough for you?" I asked, not bothering to hide my anger.

"It's not like it matters. We haven't exactly had a huge success rate," she muttered, looking back at the door.

"I guess I'll just have to find some way to have fun around here," she added as she walked away shrugging her shoulders.

As soon as Jane was out of sight, I turned back to the door. Luckily I didn't have to wait long before the door opened. And there she was. She looked more incredulous than scared. I was happy to see that she seemed to have a better grip on the situation than most of the girls before her had.

She stopped walking as she caught sight of me, probably thinking I was just another loony. And then she did something that completely surprised me. She held her hand out and introduced herself—a completely normal act in a completely unreal situation.

"Hi, I'm Ally," she began. She seemed cool and collected, but the second she started talking, I could see right through her.

"David," I introduced myself, noticing a small tremor in her hand.

Maybe she thought we were all crazy. I looked at her, trying to peg her. Maybe she thought she better go along with our explanations rather than risk ending up on the ten o'clock news as the poor teenage girl found mutilated by the side of the road.

I glanced at John, wondering if he was ready to introduce a new member into the household.

"So, David, are you crazy too?" She said with a half-joking tone. She looked almost hopeful. She was probably praying that I would tell her that Jane and John were in fact insane and that I could lead her to the nearest exit without delay.

"Well, none of us are crazy, except maybe Jane. It's true that we can't leave, and we can't die. You could try to leave. I could show you to the door, but I promise you that you won't get very far. Not that we would stop you or anything," I added, hoping that she didn't assume the worst of us when I said she wouldn't get very far.

"Oh. Would it be okay if I just met everyone else living here first?"

As surprised as she looked that I had actually offered to show her the way out, her response surprised me even more. She wasn't even going to try to leave. That had to be a first.

"Sure, no problem," I said with more excitement than I'd felt since I'd entered the house.

Ally

David showed me around the house pointing out places that were too dangerous for a "newcomer like me." John's room, the laundry room, and the guest room were almost completely safe. I guess it made sense that they kept their new guests in the safest room. Although, according to them, there was no such thing as a guest. Once someone was in, there was no way out.

I found myself trusting David, and even though I felt extremely idiotic, I felt an immediate connection with him. When I first saw him, adrenaline began coursing through my veins. I could feel my heart pounding and my hands shake, a sign that most people interpreted as fear. The only thing I felt at that moment however was excitement. Great, I was stuck in a house with a bunch of loonies, and the only reason I didn't want to leave immediately was because of a crush on a guy that I'd only known for five minutes, and the promise of an adventure I had dreamed of compared to the endless cycle of homework, tests, and work.

I snapped out of my reverie when David led me into the guest room. The room was amazing and, once again, bigger than I could've possibly imagined. There were three bunk beds to the left of the door and a dresser against the wall to the right of the door. The mattresses on the bunk beds were draped with colorful sleeping bags. I wondered idly if anyone else slept in there.

"So are any of these beds taken?" I asked, trying to figure out which one I wanted. I immediately ruled out three of the mattresses since they were on the top bunks. Sometimes I walked in my sleep, and I did not want to wake up in the middle of the night after doing a five-foot nose dive.

"No, there's no one staying in this room at the moment." John supplied. "Michelle and Eric stay in a room on the other side of the house, and I'm not really sure where Leslie and Sam are because they tend to keep to themselves. Any bed you want is yours."

I nodded absently and waited for the tour to commence.

The other two bedrooms were pronounced off-limits for the time being. Apparently they wouldn't allow me into the dangerous rooms until I was a true believer.

"We only let those that believe something truly awful could happen to them go into those rooms. Once you understand the dangers behind these doors, you'll be ready to take the care necessary to go inside," John explained.

I nodded, starting to feel like a bobble-head and thinking that if John and the others were in fact insane, they wouldn't have much trouble rigging the place themselves. There actually was a very good possibility that the house was dangerous.

I was led along the hallway, keeping away from the walls as instructed. We passed a few hallways that branched off, all of which I was instructed to keep away from as well. Of course that instruction nagged at me, making me want to explore every square inch. Finally we made our way back to the marble staircase. It was tempting to run down those stairs, making a mad dive for the door. I was pretty sure David and John expected me to do so because of the way they looked at me. They didn't seem prepared to stop me either.

I took a deep breath and kept walking. And as I did so an identical look of surprise, mouth hanging open and everything, spread across their faces. I laughed and shrugged.

"As long as you're not going to kill me or torture me, I have nowhere to go," I confessed. Before they could try to comfort me or give me their pity I started to walk forward again. But before I could get very far, someone grabbed the collar of my shirt and pulled me back. I ran into David, who I assumed was the one that pulled me back just in time to see the hallway light fall onto the floor and shatter into shiny shards. That definitely would've ended with a trip to the emergency room.

I looked up and saw that the entire ceiling was lined with lights. They almost looked like icicles. When I looked back to the floor though, the shards were gone. I looked back up at the ceiling. None of the lights were missing!

"That was your first lesson and definitely not your last," John said. "I know you probably don't believe us yet, but that couldn't have hurt our case."

"No, definitely not," I whispered. I was still hanging on to David, unable to control my breathing. I glanced up at his face, and we exchanged an awkward look while I came to my senses and released him from my death grip.

I didn't really want to let go. Having someone to hold on to was a good feeling, but I couldn't imagine that David wanted a pathetic, terrified girl clinging to his arm.

"All right, well, we can go into the kitchen now. It's the only room past all the hallways. I'm sure at least Michelle and Eric will be sitting down for dinner now. Just stay away from the stove okay? And until we can get you more adapted to this place, please don't go anywhere else without asking first."

"Okay," I agreed, not prepared for another demonstration.

"And then after dinner, I can show you the gym!" David told me enthusiastically. "It's a great way to get away."

The two people in the room looked up at me when I walked into the room. I felt like a new pet being paraded around. I had been informed that there were four people other than John, David, and Jane. There was an incredibly skinny Asian woman with straight black hair and deep sea-green eyes caught in the middle of a smile. The smile was probably put on her face by the man she was sitting next to. Her left leg was woven around his right leg and he also had been smiling. However once they registered the fact that a stranger had just entered their house, the smiles fled from their faces.

"Ally, this is Michelle and Eric. Michelle and Eric, this is Ally." John made the formal introductions and then gave me a nudge into the room. David left with John muttering that they needed a moment alone to talk, and I was on my own.

I stood there awkwardly, searching for anything that I could say. *Hey, guys, it's nice to be here. I enjoy the company of lunatics.* Yeah, that would go over really well. Or maybe, *So how many times have you died?* I was definitely out of my league.

Luckily Michelle stood up before the moment turned too awkward and held out her hand for me to shake. I grabbed it like a life line and couldn't help from smiling at her small act of kindness.

"I know you probably feel like your world is falling apart right now," Michelle began. "But we all look out for each other in this house, especially for the new people. You're gonna be just fine, honey."

She was the most reassuring person I had met yet. She had that air of openness and trustworthiness about her.

"Thanks," I said, suddenly shy. I looked toward Eric wondering what to expect from him. I noticed a wedding ring on Michelle's hand and assumed that the two of them were married.

"You're probably starving by now," Michelle prompted. "Let me get something together for you."

"Oh, no, I'm fine," I protested weakly, but as soon as I stopped talking my stomach let out a loud gurgle which caused both of them to laugh.

"It's really no bother." Michelle really was soothing. I could already tell that everyone probably went to her with their problems. I assumed she talked with Grumpy every day. Or maybe the reason Jane was so grumpy was that she didn't spend enough time with Michelle.

"Unfortunately the spaghetti was knocked all over the floor during a disagreement earlier, but we do have some left over pizza from this afternoon."

"Pizza would be great."

I tried to smile but the effort fell flat. Michelle didn't seem to notice, and I was grateful. Eric was watching me though and I probably would've run out of the room if it weren't for Michelle. I stared back, waiting for him to lower his gaze. Instead he grinned and offered his hand.

"Ya gotta have the balls to stand up for yourself here. Especially with Jane," he added in a Brooklyn-type accent that threw me off guard. "Let that be your first lesson. You didn't let me stare you down. Good job."

I stared down at his arms as I grasped his hand, noticing the tattoo sleeve that resembled a page from a Magic Eye book. He might have been tough and extremely intimidating, but he seemed like a good guy. But then again, like I said, my first impressions suck.

"Don't pay any attention to him, Ally. He's really just a big teddy bear at heart, all talk." Michelle handed me the plate of pepperoni pizza, giving Eric a mock punch to the shoulder.

I greedily took a huge bite, realizing my mistake too late. The hot cheese burned the top of my mouth, and I had to open my mouth, putting my hand in front of my open lips to let some of the heat escape and avoid the embarrassment of spitting a chunk of pizza onto the plate. I hoped to at least maintain the charade that I wasn't completely clumsy for a few days.

Finally the burning subsided, and I could swallow the piece. I took a big gulp of the water that Michelle had placed next to me while I had been distracted with the scalding hot pizza. Once the pizza cooled off, I quickly finished my slice and sat at the table, contemplating my situation. It could have actually been a blessing in disguise. So what if they were a little coo coo for cocoa puffs; at least they treated me with more respect than my own mother.

I continued to mull over my options, not even realizing that Michelle and Eric had said their good-byes. Great, I'd probably already come off as rude and inconsiderate, completely ignoring the couple as they left.

While I sat there upsetting myself even more, David snuck up behind me. I really needed to pay more attention.

"Hey! I want to show you the most awesome place in the house." His eyes actually sparkled with excitement, something that I had always assumed was just a figure of speech and nothing more. With David, I could actually see the gleam.

"All right, let's go." I couldn't help but smile at his enthusiasm. I almost forgot the crazy events of the past few hours as I let David eagerly lead the way.

David

I led the way to the gym in silence. I knew that I had a job to do, but we had failed so many times before that I found myself giving up. A part of me just wanted to enjoy Ally's company. That shouldn't have scared me so much compared to what the other part of me had done to the other girls that had been chosen. Had they been chosen, or just unlucky enough to be in the wrong place at the wrong time? I was unsure about how the whole process worked. As I thought about it, the whole process didn't work.

I glanced back at Ally, trying to get the cheerful look and tone just right. I had welcomed seven girls into the house in exactly the same way for the past five years. It hadn't always been the right approach, but opening myself up seemed to give them the courage to open up to me.

I thought back to Jane's face as I had asked her if Ally wasn't pretty enough for her. It dawned on me that perhaps Ally was too pretty. Each time I had worked my way into the hearts of the six other girls (one girl had rejected me completely), it took its toll on Jane. She couldn't stand to see me with other people, even if it was for the sake of the cause and nothing more. We would inevitably fight and break up, and once the girl was gone, Jane would forgive me. Jane would apologize for being so jealous, and I would apologize even though everything I did was for her.

Ally glanced at me, looking away quickly. My thoughts had escaped to my face, and I realized that I had been staring at her intensely. If she asked, I could play it off as infatuation but I was tired of playing the part.

"Sorry," I apologized, not giving her the chance to ask. "I was lost in thought," I confessed truthfully.

"I understand," she laughed, genuinely. "Happens to me all the time," she admitted. "In fact Michelle and Eric probably think I'm pretty rude right about now. I didn't even hear them say good-bye I was so deep in thought." She bit her lip, embarrassed.

Too tired to put up the charade any longer, I decided that honesty would be my new policy. Not complete honesty, but I wouldn't outright lie to her. I would only lie by omission.

"Sometimes I feel like I run through everything in my head before I actually say anything," I admitted. "It can get pretty tiring, editing everything before you speak."

"I know what you mean!" she exclaimed. She smiled brightly as we entered the gym.

Ally

David took me to the gym just like he promised. He showed me a safe place to get changed into some workout clothes that he had found for me. As I changed into the shorts, t-shirt, and tennis shoes, I found myself surprised that they were the right size. I would have to ask David where everyone got their clothes. I walked out of the changing room and spotted David stretching beside the track. For a supposedly cursed house, it was the coolest place I had ever walked into.

"So what do you want to do?" David asked excitedly. "Do you run? Walk? How about playing soccer, basketball, or tennis? Oh, I forgot to ask if you wanted to go swimming. I should've thought of that before I took you here. The pool is underneath the tennis court!" He exclaimed, already jogging in place to warm up.

"I think I'll just go for a run." I was itching to play soccer, but I liked playing with more people.

"Okay, I'll come with. How far do you usually go?"

"About four miles," I replied absent mindedly.

"Phew. Guess I'll have to try to keep up." He looked daunted by the task.

"I haven't run in a while though," I added, trying to make him feel better.

I fell into the rhythm of running pretty easily. I powered through the first mile with no trouble other than the initial awkwardness caused by running next to David. After the second mile, I left David behind as he stopped and sat beside the track. At first I felt self-conscious, wondering if he was watching me, but when I looked back over, he was looking to the entrance of the gym. Jane had decided to grace us with her presence. Wonderful.

As I finished another lap, David stopped me.

"Hey, Ally, I'm going to go get us some water. I'll be back in a minute." He sounded way too tense, and since I wasn't dense, I figured he was fleeing from Jane. There went the notion of my own personal bodyguard. Oddly, Jane the bully scared me more than a creepy trap-filled house.

"Okay, I'll just finish up while you're gone." I decided to keep running. I didn't have to acknowledge Jane until David was back. The reasoning didn't stop the stab of betrayal though. So what if David didn't want to be around Jane. He obviously didn't feel comfortable around Jane, and he had left me alone with her.

I smiled my unconvincing smile and ran off, not waiting for David to say good-bye. Maybe if I got back into running before David left, then Jane wouldn't approach me.

Luckily Jane wasn't in the mood to run. Out of the corner of my eye, I noticed that she had headed toward the weights. Falling back into my rhythm, I lost track of time and before I knew it, I had run a record seven miles. I guess David must've gotten sidetracked.

David

I left the gym as I had always done, knowing the exact outcome that would follow. I felt a twinge of guilt as Ally tried her best to give me a convincing smile. Jane had never made any of the girls feel particularly safe. She took vicious satisfaction in making them feel self-conscious and uncomfortable.

I walked back to the kitchen feeling the weight of our work pulling me down until my head actually hung. I sat at the kitchen table with Michelle and Eric. They had left after Ally finished eating as they always had done. Then we sat and waited to see the potential of the new girl.

No one would speak until it was over. The room was heavy with unspoken emotion and dark with our tainted consciences. We couldn't even look at each other. I crossed my arms staring at the wall and mulling over my actions. I didn't want to be the bad guy anymore. I desperately tried to think of a way, any way, to put the usual chain of events to a stop. No matter what I did, in the end it all came down to Jane.

Ally

I walked into the bathroom locking the door behind me. I knew that I wasn't supposed to wander around the house without anyone showing me the safest routes to the safest rooms. I had already been shown the bathroom though so I was stupidly confident; at least that I wouldn't burst into flames as I started the shower and began to take my clothes off. I felt like an eight-year-old on a field trip. I probably couldn't have walked three steps before someone was beside me asking where I was going. Then that someone would follow me the entire way.

I guess I was lucky after all that David had wimped out on me. I wanted to slip away before he got back, but I definitely didn't want to end up dead in some kind of freak accident. I still didn't believe that people couldn't die in the house, but I had encountered at least one chilling close call to death, or at least dismemberment that I wouldn't consider exploring a room by myself. The fact that I didn't believe people couldn't die was probably a great motivating force behind allowing David to lead me around like a puppy.

Throughout the run, I had begun to sweat like a pig, and after standing still, the sweat basically poured off me which made me feel completely unattractive. That's when I thought about the bathroom that John had shown me earlier. Unfortunately I had never used the shower before. But then again, what trap could have possibly been waiting for me in there? Boiling hot water? I could check that before I stepped into the bathtub. The shower head strangling me? Okay, the house was weird, but that seemed a little farfetched. I'd seen the lights in the hallway fall but I couldn't imagine the shower head creeping toward me like a boa constrictor and wrapping itself around my neck.

I stood there debating whether or not I should wait for David or take a shower. Not waiting seemed more appealing because one, David was hot and I was not as I continued to sweat, and two, no one was going to watch me take a shower like they had watched me do just about everything else. Then I noticed Grumpy walking toward me.

I was surprised because instead of wearing her initial I'm-so-pissed-at-the-world face, she actually looked like she was about to start a conversation with me.

"Wow you're sweating like an old, fat man who just got done running a marathon," she laughed checking me out from head to toe. It was conversation; it just wasn't the pleasant, if not awkward, ice-breaker type that I had been hoping for.

"You would be too if you'd just run seven miles," I answered feeling very defensive. I wasn't in the mood to make enemies. Seriously, in my opinion, high school never ends. I thought that I would leave the cliques and the bratty girls behind when I graduated. I thought college would be filled with open-minded, intellectual people who welcomed new students with open arms. Instead I found sororities and fraternities that basically acted the part of the "populars."

I'm not saying I was a nerd. I'm sure dork would fit my personality better though. Just the fact that I'm making that distinction tells anyone that I don't fall in the cool, popular category. I read a lot of books, so many books that I had not one, but two bookshelves lining the walls of my bedroom. I was in the band. All someone has to do to make people think, "Wow, what a dork," is say, "I was in the band." The especially vulnerable band geeks were girls that played "manly" instruments like trombone and boys that played "girly" instruments like flute. Now, no one can accuse me of being mean; that was just how I saw it in the way those students were treated. And before anyone accuses me of picking on any of those students by even thinking they were dorks or accuses me of not knowing what I'm talking about, I was the girl that played the tuba.

"Okay, wow," Jane disrupted my thoughts. "Earth to Ally!"

"Oh, sorry, mean people bore me." It felt amazing to finally stand up to Jane. But then I started thinking about all the excuses she could have had for being such a *grumplefrump*, my personal word for grumpy, snotty people. She could have been separated from her family. She could have had a really hard time adjusting to living in that insane place. I never even asked her how she ended up there. Before I could try to make amends though, she was back in attack mode.

"Yeah, whatever, that hurt so much. Anyway, as I was saying, just go take a shower already. You stink."

"I'm not supposed to go anywhere by myself," I answered, feeling like a dorky teenage girl that was being peer pressured into skipping school but wimped out and completely annihilated any chance she had at acceptance. Actually, that was kind of exactly what I was doing. Except, I didn't think skipping school usually lead to the possibility of death.

"All right, Miss goody two shoes, go ahead and look like hell for your new boy toy for all I care," she countered, putting her hand on her hip and giving me an I'm-so-superior-to-you look.

"He's not my boy toy!" I defended myself, feeling a flush of anger rising up into my cheeks. I just loved looking embarrassed when I was really just flat out pissed. "We just met today. If anything, we're just friends." I continued pathetically. Almost everyone that went to high school knew someone that insisted she was just friends with a guy and then a week later, they were sucking face in the hallway.

"Like I care. All I'm saying is have fun looking *fugly* in front of the only hottie in this place." And then she walked away swinging her hips side to side in an obviously purposeful manner. She thought she was so cool. But if I had to be honest to myself, she was probably a whole hell of a lot cooler than I was.

So feeling like a loser, I decided to prove to myself that I was a confident, capable person who was definitely not a goody two shoes and go take a shower by myself. Then I immediately thought that my entire thought process was a complete oxymoron. Taking a shower alone seemed to be the exact definition of goody two shoes. But I was still breaking the rules, as claustrophobic as they had started to make me and it felt like I could breathe again.

So turning my thought process back to the steaming shower running in front of me, I checked the temperature to make sure the water wouldn't boil me alive and then checked to see if the shower head would come out. Even though I doubted the cord would strangle me, I didn't want to feel paranoid throughout the entire shower. I just wanted to relax and let the warm water work out all the kinks that had started building up since that creepy dream. Sure I could've used the sink to wash myself, but the shower felt so much better. Last, I checked for towels because even though the embarrassment wouldn't kill me, it would still leave its mark.

After stepping into the shower and closing the glass door behind me with a *click*, I immediately began leaning against the shower wall and letting the stream of hot, glorious water flow over me. I found the shampoo and began washing out my hair. Everything felt so good that I managed to let myself go and began daydreaming that it was just a normal shower in a normal house. By the time I was in full relaxation mode, I began to feel the water rising up to my ankles.

Upset that my shower was going to be cut short by a clogged drain, I turned around and checked to see if there were any nasty hairballs stuck in the drain. Being the total idiot that I was, I hadn't realized that I forgot to open the drain before starting my shower. I bent down to unplug the drain but the chain broke off the plug, forcing me to try to get the plug out without any leverage.

As the water reached my lower calves, I went to turn off the water. I turned the knobs for the cold and hot water at the same time—I'd had one too many experiences of either scalding myself or freezing myself—and each knob broke off and fell into the water with a *plop*. I was virtually destroying the shower with each attempt I made. I could just imagine Jane huffing about the destruction of the only thing in the place that made her happy. Even if she didn't care about the shower, she would have loved to complain about my blunder.

So finally, I decided that I had to get out of the shower and find someone to help me. Maybe they had some kind of wrench that they could use to turn the knobs. Again I turned my anti-Midas touch to the handle of the glass door which also broke off and fell into the water. With a sinking feeling, the realization hit me that the consecutive break down of the drain, the shower knobs, and the door handle could not possibly be just mere coincidence. And for what must have been the billionth time in just hours, I smacked myself on the forehead.

Jane hadn't told me which shower was safe to use, and knowing her she had probably done it on purpose. She probably would've given me the thumbs-up even if I would've asked her. Either that or she would've told me in her snarky voice that I could figure it out myself.

So putting my anger at her and myself aside, I began trying everything I could possibly think of to get out of my predicament. The glass door had latched into place making it impossible for me to turn once I had broken the handle off.

I looked up to see if there was enough space between the top of the glass door and the ceiling for me to wedge myself through. If I was even going to try to give that option a shot though I had to wait until the water reached a higher level. I didn't even want to think about that though. I banged on the glass door, not deluding myself for a second in thinking that it would actually break. With a sigh of defeat, knowing that I was going to be embarrassed after all, I took a big breath and began yelling for help.

"Please let it be Michelle," I pleaded to anyone up there that would listen. I guess even Jane would have been okay at that point. I definitely didn't want to be rescued by one of the guys. I'm not a prude, but I didn't like the idea of a guy I barely knew getting the full frontal of my ta-tas and what-not. I wasn't exactly in the position to be picky about my savior though because at that point, the water was up to my waist and was definitely not going anywhere but up.

"Ally? Ally, is that you in there?" David shouted through the door. Of course David would be the one to burst in there and see me completely naked. But first it seemed that he had to get past the bathroom door. It sounded like he was doing everything to kick down that big oak door but I didn't think that even the Incredible Hulk could save me at that point. The water reached my neck and then completely engulfed me. I paddled as hard as I could to stay above the water but soon I hit the top, and at that point, I could see that only a size zero, which I was most definitely not, could even dream of fitting between the gap that I had been hoping would be big enough for me.

I took one last deep breath as the water reached the top and began splashing onto the floor. I remembered hearing accounts of survivors that had been resuscitated after drowning. Maybe it was peaceful like they said. I always thought drowning would be an unbearable way to go, almost like an extreme, deathly case of claustrophobia.

As I began to feel light-headed, not daring to take that gulp of air that I so desperately needed but couldn't take, I saw David break through the door at last. He had actually used an ax on the door handle. My lungs were screaming at me in agony, desperate for even just a few molecules of oxygen, but as David ran into the room, slipping on the water I felt like everything might be okay. That was probably the lack of oxygen, muddling my brain as I lost consciousness.

David

I finally found the common sense to use an ax on the bathroom door after a few minutes of ineffective pounding. I worried the whole way as I ran to the basement and into the tool room.

"This is not the proper protocol!" John yelled, trying to get in my way.

"Maybe it should be!" I shouted back, pushing him to the side.

I knew that I shouldn't attempt to save Ally. That one action went against every rule that we had put in place from the start of our *captivity*. I don't know what force drove me to the role of knight in shining armor, a position I had never imagined myself in, but it kept me moving even when my brain was telling me to stop. I just couldn't stand sitting at that table anymore, knowing the exact consequences of my actions. I had entered the unknown, and although fear coursed through me, I was strangely exhilarated by my choice.

I would have sprinted past the saw, yet another trap in the hell house of endless dangers, but my need to get back to Ally in time kept me cautious. I could not afford to waste the time needed to reappear at the base of the stairs after dying. I grabbed the ax and began running back to the bathroom, leaving a wide space between the saw and myself.

When I reached the bathroom door, I didn't break my stride as I swung the ax at the thick, menacing door. I was a few swings from breaking the door down when I heard the water begin to hit the floor like a miniature waterfall. I braced myself for one last hard swing and managed to break through to the other side.

Running into the bathroom was like trying to run down a Slip 'n Slide. As soon as I hit the water I fell backward, knocking my head against the tile floor. Standing up, I began seeing spots that cleared to give way to Ally floating unconsciously in the water. I scrambled for the doorknob, forgetting that Ally had probably already broken the handle from the inside. Without thought, I swung the ax toward the door, fracturing the glass into a million little pieces and causing a wave of water and broken glass to come crashing down on me.

I held on to the bathroom sink, bracing myself against the torrent, feeling the sharp bits of glass biting against my skin as I tried to pull myself closer to the shower. Suddenly Ally slid out of the shower, riding on the wave and slamming right into me. Finally I could allow the water to carry me out of the bathroom as I held on to Ally's arm, making an effort to keep my eyes elsewhere.

I put my ear to her mouth, checking to see if she was still breathing. She wasn't. My mind began to race as I fought off blind panic. I had never done CPR before. Sure, John was a doctor, but that didn't mean he had shown me anything. His job wasn't to save our lives unfortunately, and the most I could do for anyone was offer to put a band-aid on a small cut. So mimicking the CPR that all the doctors on television did, I put my hands together and began pushing against her chest in even beats. I felt the crack before I even heard it, jumping back with a gasp. I had broken one of her ribs! I didn't even want to consider continuing when, with a sputter, Ally began coughing up water and gasping for breath.

I quickly covered Ally with a soaked towel that I found a few feet away.

"Try to hold still, I think I might have broken one of your ribs," I pleaded, feeling myself cringe in guilt as I thought about hurting her. It had worked though; I had saved her life.

Everyone else would probably say that saving Ally was just a waste of time and that sooner or later she wouldn't escape. That may have been the case, but something needed to change.

Sure, each time someone new came into our ranks, we watched them for a few weeks and showed them all the dangers we knew, but we just accepted that sooner or later, each of us had to experience death. But what if each death really did take away from us, if only a little bit at a time? Ally was so alive that she made me feel like a ghost.

"Oh god," she rasped, looking at me in horror. I was lost, thinking that maybe I had hurt her more than I realized.

"Are you okay? I'm so sorry! I didn't mean to hurt you, I swear. I just . . . I just needed to get you breathing again."

I raced to explain myself, watching her face go from horror to avoidance.

"Ally, please say something," I pleaded trying to catch her eyes with mine.

"I'm okay, really. I just need some clothes, please."

She looked away, dropping her voice to a low mumble toward the end.

"Oh, of course, I'm sorry. I just needed to get you breathing," I repeated. "Your clothes are kind of soaked, but I can go find you some new ones."

I got up to leave, hoping that no one would find her lying on the floor like that, but before I could stand up she grabbed my wrist.

"No, please don't go," she pleaded, gripping my wrist tighter and tighter. "I'm such an idiot. I shouldn't have left without you. I'm just getting so tired of feeling like a child. My parents watched me nonstop and now you all do too. I feel like the only reason you even want to hang out with me is because I'm new and you have to."

She blurted her thoughts out in a breathless rush avoiding eye contact with me and taking small, shallow breaths. I could only imagine how much her chest was hurting her.

"I can see why you thought that I was taking care of you out of obligation. I have been a bit overbearing," I began, trying to hide the guilt I felt over leaving her to Jane. "And you are right. I would look after anyone that was new to the house. But I wouldn't feel like I do now. I probably wouldn't have hacked the door to pieces for anyone else. I don't want you to get hurt, Ally. Well, I don't want anyone here to get hurt. But I can't stand to see you in danger. You just don't belong here." I was already saying too much.

"Are you saying you don't want me here?" She looked truly hurt, and I immediately regretted the way I chose to phrase my explanation.

"No! Well, yes and no. I don't want you here, because I don't want you to get hurt. But selfishly, I do want you here because somehow you've managed to breathe life back into this place, and into me."

I felt the corny words leave my lips and was surprised to realize that there was actually some truth behind them.

Ally

After letting a bombshell of a confession about the importance of my presence to him after only one day (*geesh*), David had changed the subject and insisted on finding me some clothes in a nearby closet. After changing into dry clothes carefully—it still really hurt to breathe and I was beginning to believe that David actually had broken one of my ribs—I left the room and found David leaning on the rail at the top of the stairs in the main room.

He was staring at the big sun in the middle of the room.

"You know if you stare at that thing long enough, it starts to actually look like it's burning."

I jumped in surprise. I didn't think he had heard me coming.

"At least there are no ROUSs," I joked, snorting stupidly at my reference to *The Princess Bride*.

David laughed, either at my joke or my snort. I felt the hot blush spread across my cheeks. Still, I couldn't stop smiling. Somehow I couldn't stay embarrassed for long when I was around David. He made my silly notions seem relevant, if not justifiable.

"What's an ROUS?" he asked. So he had definitely been laughing at my snort.

"Don't tell me you haven't seen *The Princess Bride*." I gasped mockingly, holding my hand to my mouth and opening my eyes wide. I winced as a sharp pang rippled through my chest. I made a promise to myself that there would be no more gasping and no more moving my arms above my head. I was surprised my chuckle-snort hadn't caused the same amount of pain.

"Nope, can't say I have," David replied, appraising my condition as I cleared the wince from my expression

"If we ever get out of here, I am making you watch that movie. I don't care if I have to hold you down."

"You don't have to hold me down, although I really wouldn't object to that either."

He actually winked at me. Was he flirting with me? I could never tell. In high school, everyone used to accuse me of being a flirt even though I was just trying to make friends and actually have a conversation with people. God forbid that those other people belonged to the opposite sex. While I was debating whether David was flirting or just talking, I realized that he was waiting for some kind of sign that I had heard him.

"Sorry," I supplied lamely. "Sometimes my mind just takes me away."

"It's okay. So what's an ROUS?" he asked lightly, no sign of the flirtatious attitude I had thought I'd seen.

"A Rodent of Unusual Size."

"Sounds scary," he laughed. "Luckily the only animal we have is Dorothy, our pet cat."

"How did you get a pet cat? It's not like you can make a trip to the pet store." It was easy to fall into joke mode around David, but I still wondered at my surprisingly sudden and easy transition into that life.

"She just wandered in here one day back when it was only me, Jane, and John stuck here. I really believe she kept me from going crazy. But then more and more people showed up and brought the crazy back. I think you're doing for me now what Dorothy did for me then. I feel like I can be normal around you, whatever normal may be." He finished his thought keeping his eyes down on the mysterious sun.

Although I wasn't new to a loss for words, no one had ever taken them away from me like that. That strange surge of adrenaline rushed through my veins again, making my heart pound. Finally, making a point to keep my mouth from hanging open at its hinges, I started talking, not really knowing exactly what I would say.

"I can't say you bring normalcy to my life. In fact you, along with this place and everyone else in it, do quite the opposite. But despite the crazy horror movie-type scenes that seem to play out whenever I'm in the room, this situation has taken me away from a pretty bad place. Ha, listen to me, calling my life before a bad place. I bet if anyone in here heard me say that, they'd laugh in my face." I felt ridiculous. I knew I should've thought it through before I opened my mouth.

"There are a whole hell of a lot of things in this world worse than this place," David whispered quietly.

"I suppose there are. So why did you name the cat Dorothy?" I asked partially curious and mostly wanting to change our conversation to a lighter subject that didn't include my life before.

"Because we're 'not in Kansas anymore,' and sometimes I wish that this was a dream and I could just wake up." He looked at me as he spoke.

"Of course, I don't know if I would want you to just be a dream." Again he looked away, almost as if he was avoiding the eye contact that he had just sought out.

Apart from the awkwardness I felt from a guy possibly hitting on me, I knew I could like him. I had thought I was the only dork that constantly alluded to movies.

"So when does everyone go to sleep around here?" I asked, trying not to think of the possible connotations my question had right after the moment of complete openness that we had just shared.

"For right now, you'll have to stay in the guest room so you'll probably want to go to bed before everyone else if you have trouble sleeping in new places," David replied. "There aren't any clocks but we still manage to keep a mostly normal schedule around here. Anyways, the room can be kind of creepy, but I can assure you that there's absolutely nothing dangerous in there."

"That's the room there right?" I asked, pointing at the closed door and feeling like an idiot for already forgetting which room was the guest room.

"Yeah, I guess I better get going . . ." He trailed off at the end, obviously wanting me to stop him from leaving. At least I thought it was obvious. As soon as I thought he wanted me to ask him to stay, I immediately began to second guess my instincts.

I sat there debating with myself. Should I ask him to stay? Or should I just tell him good night? Whatever I planned on doing, I needed to do so quickly because I could see him starting to back up.

"Would you mind staying for a while?" I asked hesitantly, feeling my cheeks burning. Luckily though, I could always feel the blush, but it wasn't actually incredibly visible. "I just don't think that I could sleep right now."

I stopped talking as I realized that I was actually opening up to David. Well, I hadn't actually told him that I was still childishly afraid of the dark, but I had told him I didn't want to be alone. He probably thought I was just freaked out by the house.

"Sure. But first, I want John to have a look at your ribs. He's the closest thing we have to a doctor in this place." He smiled, making a shiver run through me, hot and cold at the same time.

I shook my head, trying to get rid of the flood of emotions that kept resurfacing every time David showed me any sign of attraction. It wasn't like I needed to get romantically involved with David on top of everything else that had been thrown at me. No one falls in love in a day.

"You daydream a lot don't you?" David broke into my thoughts, surprising me by his diagnosis that I had been daydreaming.

"I prefer to call it overanalyzing or maybe overthinking as I said before," I replied, feeling the burn in my cheeks again.

"Okay, fair enough." He smiled at me, not just a half-assed smirk, but a full on, Cheshire Cat grin, and I automatically smiled right back. By that point, my near-death drowning incident was miles away from my thoughts.

David

I left Ally in the guest room to go hunt down John. I checked his room first, but seeing that he wasn't there, I headed for the gym, figuring that he was probably swimming some laps before going to bed. I caught him on his way out of the main entrance, drying his hair with a towel.

"Hey, John, I need you to take a look at Ally." I kept my eyes down as the shame began to build again.

"I assume that means you were successful," he guessed.

"Yes," I answered shortly.

"Okay, lead the way," he prompted.

We walked to the guest room in silence, again avoiding the falling light and the walls that would crumble and fall to the floor at our touch. We passed the bathroom, our feet sinking into the carpet with a *squish* at each step as if we were walking through a marsh. John appraised the smashed wooden door and shook his head. Damage that we did to the house didn't go away, only the damage that the house itself did magically repaired itself.

"You actually did it." John shook his head, probably wondering why I went through such great lengths to save a girl from a death that wouldn't stick anyways.

He knocked on the guest room door and waited for a minute, finally entering after there was no response. Normally I would've waited outside until John was done with the examination, but I was afraid when Ally didn't respond. I quickly glanced at the bed hoping that a broken rib hadn't punctured her lung and caused her to die while I was off trying to find help.

But as I watched with weary eyes, I noticed that her chest had been rising and falling evenly while I was going through every anatomical possibility for Ally's death. John kneeled down next to her and tapped her shoulder, whispering in her ear to wake her. Still Ally slept, dead to the world, a metaphor that I wasn't quite comfortable with at that moment.

"I'm just going to check her out. I don't think that she would mind and I doubt that she'll wake up." He nodded at the door, and I headed out, trying to give Ally at least an ounce of privacy. As I opened the door, I glanced back, noticing the huge bruise that had spread beneath Ally's bra. I sucked in a deep breath and left the room quickly, not daring to look at the rest of the damage that I had inflicted upon her.

I waited out in the hallway, holding my head in my hands. If I hadn't been such a baby I could've prevented the whole thing. Jane had entered the gym and, like always, I took off running. There was so much history trapped within those walls, history that I had finally had the courage to keep from repeating itself.

When John finally opened the door, I snapped my head up, anxious to hear how she was doing.

"Is she okay?" It would have been painfully ironic if I had signed Ally's death warrant by saving her from drowning.

"She'll be fine. Although I don't think that her ribs are broken, they're definitely bruised, if not sprained. She's going to need to take it very easy for a few weeks. I would even suggest that she stay in bed for a day or two." He rubbed his eyes tiredly, shaking his head.

"I know that I shouldn't have done it," I confessed. "But I couldn't help it. And yes, I know I can't do CPR, but why do we have to assume that succumbing to a death trap is the only option inside this house?"

I spoke my thoughts in a rush, not caring whether or not John would understand.

"Well, for starters, I would have to say that you did CPR very well actually. Most people get cracked or bruised ribs from CPR. It's not very uncommon." He patted me on the shoulder, trying to comfort me. But I could still see his next comments coming as he took a deep breath and prepared to launch into one of his speeches, explaining that there was nothing we could do.

"Just don't beat yourself up about this okay? You can't be everywhere at once, and this is bound to happen again. I understand if you feel that you have to do this. But please remember that sooner or later, it has to happen."

Although he had characteristically maintained the fact that *accidents* were inevitable, he actually hadn't brushed off my need to protect Ally as silly or useless. And instead of pity, I sensed a deep sense of guilt. That guilt emanated from him periodically, which I could understand when he spoke of everyone being trapped there.

"I should feel guilty, John. I left Ally alone with Jane." I grabbed his shoulder like a life line.

"You did what you had to," he replied simply.

"Since when did all of this become a necessity?" I asked, beginning to get frustrated at our impossible situation.

"Don't forget what's going on out there," he insisted, looking as defeated as I felt.

"Fine." My shoulders slumped as the fight completely fled from me. "I'm staying in the guest room with Ally tonight. I wouldn't want Jane to come finish the job." I glared up at him defiantly, daring him to say something.

"Get some rest. Tomorrow's going to be a long day." He nodded at me and walked to his room, shutting the door behind him.

I stood there for a moment, wondering if John had just allowed me to spend the night in a room with a new girl that easily. Granted, that girl had bruised ribs and was currently so exhausted that she had slept through an examination of her sprained ribs, but I still had to go over the conversation in my head again to actually believe his acceptance. I tried not to imagine what would happen if Jane found out.

Finally, I walked into the room still shaking my head. I jumped when I saw Ally sitting up in bed staring at the door. Apparently she wasn't dead to the world after all.

David

"Sorry, I didn't mean to wake you up." I started to explain, but she didn't even seem to be looking at me. I had walked toward her when I noticed her sitting up in the bed, but she was still staring at the door.

"Is it safe?" She held out her hands, touching the air like a mime.

"Is what safe?" I sat next to her, putting my hand on her shoulder in an attempt at a comforting gesture. "Did you hear us talking? Don't worry, Jane might seem crazy, but you'll be okay for now." I watched Ally with a mixture of curiosity and caution, unsure of my next words. She began to shiver, and I reached for a blanket.

"It's hot," she said, continuing to shiver.

"Get me out!" she yelled, finally looking at me.

"Ally, it's not hot, you're freezing cold. Ally?" I shook her lightly, trying not to hurt her ribs. She looked at me again, still fearful but more trusting.

"Thank you." She muttered a few more unintelligible syllables and curled up into a ball, resting her head on my lap. She sighed and once again relaxed into the closest thing I've ever seen to a coma.

I chuckled quietly, trying to keep my voice down. I'd never actually witnessed a person sleep talking before. I didn't even realize that she was still sleeping. I suppose her comments were somewhat unintelligible, and she had been mumbling quite a bit. Then, a chilling thought crept into my mind. I could just picture her walking down the hallway and being smashed by a light fixture or falling down the stairs, burning up in the sun if she didn't break her neck first.

I stood up quickly, pacing the width of the room back and forth. I cursed to myself as I tried to snap out of it. Sure, she might have had some feelings for me, but my feelings of tenderness toward her were not supposed to be possible. I had gotten so used to being dead inside that I had forgotten how it felt to care for someone. I couldn't even remember the last time I had truly felt for Jane.

Jane. She would be wondering where I was. Someone had probably told her about my heroics. Another fight would soon follow. A fight that I didn't want Ally involved in. I thought about getting it over with while Ally was asleep, but my cowardice trapped me in the guest room.

Suddenly I didn't want to go to sleep, and I definitely didn't want to move back into my room. I wanted to watch Ally sleep to make sure that she didn't take a midnight field trip to the bottom of the swimming pool. My eyelids were making a whole different complaint though as they began to droop.

Finally I settled on repositioning Ally next to me on the bed so that I could put my arm around her. I ordered my mind to wake me up the second that I felt her move an inch, but my mind didn't really care as my head hit the pillow and my eyes snapped shut.

I dreamed of running toward someone, trying to catch her before she fell off a cliff. My feet began to sink as I ran for an eternity. I expected her to fall out of sight, but instead she fell again and again. Suddenly I was right next to her. I wrapped my arms around her, pulling her to the safety of hard ground. I brushed the hair out of her face and recognized the bitter smile on Jane's cold face.

"*You're too late,*" she cackled as she pointed to the edge of the cliff. I ran to the edge, already knowing that I would see Ally's twisted body lying at the bottom. But before I could reach the edge I felt a shove from behind, plummeting to the bottom to join Ally.

I snapped awake, my heart pounding with deep, uneven thuds. Thankfully, Ally was still lying next to me, slowly breathing in and out. Her dreams had to be more peaceful than mine which struck me as odd as I thought about the sleep talking and the events of the day. I watched her face, reveling in the complete peace; if only I could have guaranteed her that same feeling of peace when she was awake.

I brushed the hair from her face with my thumb, an impulse that I immediately regretted. I imagined Ally waking up to me leaning over her with my hand on her face after one day. She would probably think I was a creeper and try to avoid me like the plague.

I sighed and got up, figuring that sleeping in the same bed as Ally had probably also been a mistake. She was in the middle bed so I figured I would just have to settle with positioning myself in the bed between her and the door. I fell in and out of sleep imagining possible situations where Ally would be in danger, imagining myself trying to save her and, as everyone kept telling me, inevitably failing.

I must have finally drifted off during the night because when I glanced back at Ally's bed, she wasn't there anymore. I shot up, banging my head on the board above me. I panicked as every incident that I had imagined that night sprang up into my thoughts. I rolled out of bed and ran into every room checking for her. I finally reached the kitchen, stopping just outside as I heard people chattering happily. It was as if the day before had never happened.

I walked into the room, the smell of pancakes and sweet maple syrup hitting my nostrils, and braced myself for the scene before me. Jane wasn't there, which explained the pleasantness and went miles to ease me apprehension. Ally was sitting next to Michelle talking about embarrassing moments. Ally kept giggling as she tried to get through a story about a soccer practice that ended with her stepping on the ball and face-planting into a puddle.

I chuckled as I sat down across from Ally, noticing a slight twinge of pink rise up her cheeks. She threw a quick, furtive glance in my direction and then continued.

"Jess and I couldn't stop laughing for five minutes. I swear the coach thought we were delusional."

And once again Ally began to giggle. She took a few short breaths, holding her hand to her chest, but otherwise she seemed perfectly at ease.

Unfortunately, that place always seemed to take pleasure in snatching a happy moment and flushing it down the toilet. Needless to say, Jane strolled in looking like she owned the place. But when she saw the three of us sitting at the table laughing at Ally's story, she stopped and put her hands on her hips.

"Good to see you're fitting in so well," she said to Ally, ignoring the rest of us. "Like I said, as soon as you go through the whole experience of living here, you get a whole new perspective. You start to belong. Still, I think you have a lot more work to do. Maybe you could do some chores for me."

She began laughing at her disrespect, apparently oblivious to her cold reception.

"I think if you look around, you'll realize that you're the one not fitting in here." Ally shot back, making me feel pathetic for keeping silent. Apparently I could have learned a lesson from the new girl.

"Ooh, feisty are we? This is going to be more fun than I thought." Jane strolled up to the table plopping down next to me without breaking her eye contact with Ally. "You have no idea just how well I've fit in during the past few years. You know your pal, David here, dated me for a while. In fact we just broke up yesterday. Talk about a rebound." She sneered, holding her head up victoriously after jumping right into her normal dialogue. God, I was getting bored of that routine.

"Too bad you didn't show up earlier," Ally countered. "We could've eaten together. Unfortunately though, David and I have a date to get to so we'll catch ya later."

Ally popped up and grabbed my hand. She waved to Michelle and glanced at Jane with a shrug. Ally had used me to make Jane jealous, and I didn't know exactly how I felt about that. Part of me was thrilled that Jane had finally been put in her place. Part of me feared the revenge that Jane was most likely plotting right then. And part of me was afraid that Ally had no real feelings for me and never would once she was aware of some of the truth behind the relationship between me and Jane. But who was I to talk about real feelings?

Ally

I quietly led David to the gym while both my mind and pulse raced. So David had dated Jane. Not only had David dated Jane, but he had broken up with her the day that I walked in the door. Jane had said that it was his fault that she fell into the sun. Was David really a violent person? I mean, he had dated Jane and, yes, he broke up with her, but apparently that ended with her on fire. And sure, he was protecting me from Jane, but what if I needed protection from him? What if I really needed protection from everyone?

"Ally, please just talk to me. I know that you're upset. If you'll just let me explain I can clear everything up."

David held my arms, pleading with his words and his eyes.

"Hold on, please just let me think."

I didn't want to start talking until we were sitting down somewhere quiet together. I was infamous for being misunderstood and misunderstanding people in return. He nodded, and we walked the rest of the way to the gym in silence.

"The gym?" He asked, chuckling at my choice of meeting place. I couldn't help but grin, even though I was trying to keep the mood serious since I needed some serious answers.

"Well, I do go running when I need to get away from everything." I smiled as I sat down, taking a deep breath and preparing myself for the first question.

"So you dated Jane." I started. It wasn't exactly a question, but definitely required an answer.

"We've dated on and off for a while," David answered slowly, clenching his hands together.

"I'm sure that you won't have a hard time believing that she's controlling and manipulative, but she wasn't always like that." He looked up at me apologetically.

"I would've told you in time," he explained. "But we just met yesterday, and half the time your life was in danger. Telling you about that was kind of low on my list of priorities." He looked down at the floor, still blocking me out.

"I could say that I might have been more careful around Jane if you would've told me but I probably wouldn't have expected her to try to get me killed. That leads me to my next problem." I hesitated, knowing that I was about to accuse David of abuse.

"Were you responsible for Jane's accident yesterday?" I held my breath, watching David's shoulders tense.

"I broke up with Jane on the stairs, and she tried to push me down. I promise you, Ally, that Jane's accident yesterday was just that—an accident. I know that you just met me, but I promise you that I will never hurt you. You can trust me." He seemed fiercely dedicated to his promise. I wanted to believe him, but I still felt out of the loop.

"I'm sorry that I had to ask." I reached out, taking his still clenched hand in mine.

"I'm sorry that you had to hear all of that from Jane," he replied, still looking guilty.

"Well, we did just meet yesterday after all," I joked, trying to bring back a lighter atmosphere. "It's not like I've told you everything about myself. But there will be plenty of time for that." I continued, standing up and taking off my shirt to reveal my bikini underneath.

I felt light-headed and self-conscious as the blood rushed to my head. I walked toward the pool quickly, looking back before I jumped in.

"You coming?" I asked, teasingly before diving into the warm water.

I came up for air a few seconds later, feeling the pain in my chest. I paddled to the side of the pool so that I could hang on to the wall and catch my breath while searching for David. He wasn't anywhere near the pool, and I began to wonder if he had gone to change when something touched my back. I screeched and twirled around half expecting to see some kind of aquatic animal. Instead, David sprang up from underneath the water, yet again startling a squeal from me. He laughed in a way that I could only describe as a guffaw as I fought to catch my breath and slow my heart rate.

"Not funny!" I yelled, even though I was also grinning. I gave him a mock punch and in response David put his hand on his shoulder, pretending to be in pain. I went to dunk his head underwater, but he caught my arms and lifted me above the water, twirling me around until we were in the middle.

"I'll do it," he said, seriously, lifting me above the water in preparation to throw me. "I have a list of demands." He winked at me, unable to maintain the bad guy charade.

"I guess I have to meet them. I mean after all it would be a tragedy if I were thrown across the pool. Imagine the headlines—*Local Girl Refuses Demands, Suspect Throws Her into Water*. We'd be the top story." By then we were both laughing uncontrollably. I put my head too close to the water, accidentally snorting some of the pool water up my nose.

I hadn't thought about drowning in the shower while I jumped into the pool or as we joked around, but suddenly the feeling of water in my lungs caused me to lose the fragile control that I had established. I reached my arms out toward David, fighting a panic attack. Hyperventilating almost felt like drowning and I couldn't get control of myself as I began to sink.

A strong steady pair of arms lifted me up and toward the shallow end. Before I knew it, I was standing up in the water, still shaking but no longer submersed. I collapsed on the ground, my head just above the water line. David still picked me up though, looping my arms around his neck as he carried me up and out of the water. He put me down on solid ground, but I couldn't let go of him. I doubted my legs could hold me up. We stood there for a few minutes in silence until David finally broke it, pulling me away from him.

"Are you okay?" he asked, rubbing my arms as I began to shiver.

"I'm fine." I lied, already beginning to feel embarrassed for freaking out.

"I'm sorry I shouldn't even have thought about throwing you. Anyone would feel afraid. Most people wouldn't even go into the water the day after a near-drowning." He kept looking at me, waiting for some kind of response but I couldn't say anything. "I shouldn't have even let you go in there. John told me you should basically stay in bed all day and here I am going swimming with you." He shook his head, yet again blaming himself for my mistakes.

"It's not your fault," I argued.

"It was my idea," I reminded him with a wink and a smirk.

"I can't believe that you wanted to go swimming. How are you not in pain right now?" He began assessing me again like I was some kind of project. It reminded me of fifth grade home economics. We had to take an egg home for the weekend and make sure that it didn't get cracked. I had cracked my egg the very first day and spent the rest of the weekend constantly staring at it, waiting for the crack to spread and yolk to ooze out of the sides. I was David's cracked egg.

"It doesn't hurt that much." I lied, trying to seem tougher than I actually was. If I put on a brave face, maybe he wouldn't treat me like such a damsel in distress. Although if I stopped lying to myself, I had to admit that I had pretty much taken up that role the moment I walked through the door.

"All right, well, let's go get dried up." He began leading me toward the locker rooms, grabbing a towel from the rack next to the pool and draping it around my shoulders.

David

I left Ally to change in the women's locker room, mentally slapping myself. I didn't want to make excuses for my lack of good judgment, but when Ally took off her clothes, she took me by surprise. I don't want to sound like a pervert or anything, but honestly, there isn't a straight guy in the world that wouldn't have had the same response as I did. In fact, there are many straight guys that would've displayed much less self-control than I had.

I hadn't even paid much attention to the black and blue bruise in the middle of her chest as she jumped into the water. I guess that actually gave me some credit since I restrained myself from staring at her chest.

So to sum it all up, I had let Ally go into the water a day after drowning, snuck up behind her, and threatened to throw her in the middle of the deep end. And of course, she had tried to make me feel better, acting like nothing was wrong. I couldn't begin to guess at her thoughts about me.

I finished changing, still shaking my head at my stupidity. I walked out into the gym, keeping an eye out for Ally and, since fate loved being cruel, instead, I spotted Jane sitting on the bench by the track, her eyes trained on me. Whenever she caught me in her stare, I became helpless, like a soldier turned to stone under Medusa's glare.

Ally walked out just then, drying her hair with a towel. She had her head down so she didn't see Jane sitting on the bench. Instead of walking into another blunder, I steered Ally away, keeping her back turned to Jane. I would have plenty to answer for later, but right then I just wanted to prevent another disaster.

"How does some hot chocolate sound?" I asked, trying to keep my voice calm. My shoulders were tense, and my hair on end because I half expected Jane to start something even though, and perhaps because, we were completely ignoring her. I glanced back, relieved to see that she had stayed on the bench. Only her eyes followed us. She smirked and then blew me a kiss.

"Sounds great," Ally replied enthusiastically.

"I don't know how you can stay so positive," I remarked, marveling at her resilience. If I were her, I probably would have been in bed, hiding from the world.

"It's no big deal." She shrugged, shutting me out again. Ally opened the kitchen door just in time for us to find John arguing with Michelle.

"You should have told me!" Michelle yelled at John.

"What good would it have done?" John shouted back at Michelle, turning his back on her. "Ally was already safe in bed by the time I could have done anything. It was too late either way."

John backed away sitting down heavily on the bench and putting his head in his hands.

"It's all right," Ally cut in, causing Michelle to jump and excuse herself from what they had assumed was a private conversation. I just stood there with my mouth open. She didn't even know what they had been talking about. Ally walked toward John slowly, taking the place that Michelle had occupied and putting her hand on his back.

"It's not your fault either," she said, glancing at me as she spoke. The girl blew my mind. I walked out of the room before I could hear Ally excuse another stupid mistake on our part.

Michelle glared at me as I entered the hallway. She wasn't angry that no one told her about Jane's actions. She was angry because of mine.

I turned right down the long hallway and stopped at the third door on the right, my sanctuary. Instead of walking into my room and jumping into bed, maybe stopping to grab a book first, I discovered Jane lying sideways on my bed. She grinned as I entered the room. I slammed the door, ready to have a showdown and get it over with once and for all. Instead of being intimidated, she ran her hand up the side of her body, stopping at her face to put her finger in her mouth seductively.

"Could you possibly restrain yourself?" I asked in disgust, keeping my eyes trained on her face and nothing else. One false move and Jane would have gone running to Ally with some lame story about lingering feelings.

"Oh, you're no fun anymore." She actually pouted for a minute but failed to hide the still lingering gleam in her eye.

"You belong with me," she continued, sliding off the bed in one graceful, catlike move. "We both know that I have certain . . . talents," she began as she walked toward me, sliding her hand down my chest. "Talents that I'm sure that perfect little angel has never even heard of," she whispered seductively.

"Yes, because you've had so much experience in that area."

I was getting tired of Jane acting like she knew everything when she had been stuck in there, away from the rest of the world for just as long as I had. "Overall, I'm pretty sure that Ally actually knows more than you do," I reasoned.

"Maybe, but does she know more about the inner workings of this house, more about our group dynamics, or more about you? I bet she thinks you're her hero. I bet she thinks you're perfect," she continued. There was no easy solution to my problem named Jane. She nagged at me like a pesky sliver that wouldn't come out.

"I'm sure Ally's not that naïve. She actually forgave me for being stupid enough to leave her alone in a room with you though. Not a mistake I'll be making again by the way." I waited for the ultimate, inevitable comeback.

"But will she forgive you for her presence here?" she asked slyly. "Will she forgive your deception?"

"If anything, it's your fault that she's here!" I yelled at her, trying to restrain myself.

"Oh, but you helped, lover boy," she sighed her nickname for me. "You all helped."

"The line has to be drawn somewhere," I argued, sitting down on my bed. I attempted to look undefeated, but I knew the odds I was against.

She inched closer to me, taking my face in her hands and planting a long, deep kiss, exploring the inside of my mouth with her tongue. I moaned, trying to control myself. Our relationship had turned into nothing but destruction since that fateful day five years ago.

"I'm not going to listen to your manipulative nonsense any longer. Get out of my room." I turned my back on her, not caring whether or not she was about to grab my ass, push me down, or even stab me in the back. I was done being held slave to her will.

"I'm sure you'd listen if that would keep Ally safe," she whispered into my ear, stroking the back of my neck with her fingertips. Chills that had nothing to do with her touch coursed down my spine and through my body.

"You will not hurt her again." I could feel the rage boiling up inside of me. I clenched my hands, halfheartedly attempting to restrain myself.

"You don't even care about me anymore, do you?" she whimpered, shrinking into herself.

"I told you to get out of my room. If you want to talk to me again, you'll do it in front of everyone." I held the door open and stared her down, hoping that she would refuse to move and that I could physically throw her out myself. She must've gotten the message because she left without a word.

I would've loved to sit down on my bed and relax, but I figured that after throwing Jane out like that, she would be looking for more trouble. I couldn't imagine that someone was looking after Ally, so I headed back to the kitchen to see if she was still there. When I found the room empty, I walked back to the west side of the house toward the guest room.

I don't know why I didn't knock; after all the guest room was temporarily Ally's bedroom. Luckily she wasn't changing. I found her lying in bed crying into her pillow. I hesitated in the doorway, completely inept in that kind of situation. I closed the door and vowed to get Ally to tell me her true feelings, even if I also had to reveal some uncomfortable truths.

Ally

As soon as I heard the door close, I smothered the sobs in my pillow and pretended to be sleeping. I hated people to see me cry, and I refused to hear a lame speech meant to inspire me to overcome. I'd lived in the house for two long days. Didn't I deserve a few minutes to myself, a few minutes to let myself fall apart without an audience? So I pretended to be sleeping in the hopes that whoever had walked in, without even knocking, would walk away without probing me like a psychologist.

"Ally?" David whispered, sitting on the edge of my bed and rubbing my shoulder.

"Go away, David. I'm done talking about this whole mess."

I mumbled into my pillow, hoping that a huge trail of snot wouldn't gush out after the intense cry-fest I had just had.

"Would you mind if I just sit with you then? We could even talk about something else if you'd like. You know I got to hear your embarrassing story, but you never got to hear mine. That's just not fair."

"If you want to babysit me just say so. You don't have to lie." I snorted at his new and improved tactic.

"It's not like I have anywhere better to be," he insisted, just as stubbornly.

"Right, because you couldn't get away from me fast enough in the kitchen," I insisted.

"Because I didn't want to hear you continue your forgiving spree. Yeah, this place pretty much destroys a person at will, but that doesn't mean we should do the same to each other." His argument sounded rehearsed, convincing me that he'd debated that point on more than one occasion.

"Okay, so what did John and Michelle do wrong that I can't try to comfort them?"

"They both act like we all need to work together and look out for each other, but when Jane pulls a stunt like telling you to take a shower, or *inadvertently* causing an *accident*, they don't do anything." He put air quotes around his sarcasm-laden words, finally dropping his arms to his side with an exasperated sigh of defeat.

"So what would you suggest they do?" I asked, trying not to sound combative since I really was curious about his potential solution.

"I don't know," he began, looking at the floor. "It's not like we can lock her up. We're already locked up. And I mean, I guess that we can isolate ourselves from Jane. I'm sure you've noticed that our two mystery tenants, Sam and Leslie, are never anywhere to be seen. They got fed up with the drama and moved to the back of the house." He stopped, considering that option.

"That might work for Sam and Leslie, but something tells me that they don't interest Jane as much as you or I do. We're trapped inside of a house that will chew us up and spit us out with the slightest misstep but we're afraid of one delusional girl."

I laughed, suddenly feeling ridiculous for fearing Jane. I had been thrown into a death trap of a house, I had come close to death, and I had seen things that challenged my beliefs and made me question my sanity, but there I was afraid of a jealous ex-girlfriend.

"Are you really not afraid of her?" David let out a small chuckle, staring at me with wide eyes.

"Are you?" I asked, unable to believe that someone like David would be afraid of Jane.

"I'm afraid of what might happen to you," he answered, all trace of a smile gone from his face.

"Well, if you haven't been lying to me, we can't die. So what's to fear?" I kept my face down, trying to hide the very real fear bubbling up inside of me. I was afraid of the pain she could cause, and I still was afraid of dying.

"I may not die, but I do feel. I feel the pain again and again, and after all this time, a longing for the release of death nags at me." He spoke quietly. If he was a normal guy in a normal setting, I would've put him on suicide watch.

"We'll get out of here," I insisted, trying to pull him out of his depression.

"Maybe," he replied. His voice was laced with doubt and despair.

"You've already told me that no one can walk out the front door, but have you tried anything else? Have you tried the windows? Or have you found any other possible exits?" I prodded, trying to formulate a plan of escape.

"We've tried everything!" He threw up his hands in defeat.

"I'll bet you a million dollars that we'll get out." I nudged his shoulder with my arm, refusing to let him wallow in his grief when he was the one that had interrupted my pity party just a few minutes before.

"What good would a million dollars do me in here?" He asked seriously.

"Okay, so what would do you some good in here?" I asked, also completely seriously.

"A million dates would," he answered after pausing to think. He looked up at me then, studying my face while I formulated an answer. I wanted to plan my response instead of babbling on like an idiot.

"You're not afraid you'd get tired or bored of me after the first hundred or so?" I joked with him, stalling for time.

"Something tells me that you'll continue to surprise me even after a thousand dates," he answered. I imagined him leaning over to kiss me as my heartbeat sped up and then shook myself. We had known each other for two days. If I liked the guy I would date him and get to know him. I refused to start making out with a guy I barely knew in my bed. Still, I guess it didn't hurt to fantasize.

"All right, I'll bet you a million dates," I promised. I extended my hand out, intending for us to shake on the bet. Instead he took my hand and kissed the back of it. I tried to keep a straight face, but I couldn't hold in the snicker that escaped.

"What?" he asked, looking confused and slightly offended.

"That was kind of corny." I hoped that I hadn't hurt his feelings even as I continued to laugh.

"What's next, a respectful bow?" I asked, regretting my jab the instant it left my mouth.

"If that would please, m'lady," he joked as he stood up and gave me the most exaggerated bow I had ever seen. Pretty soon, we were both rolling on the floor laughing and as tears began to spill from my eyes, I tried to remember the last time I had had such fun. David regained his composure before I did.

"Of course there is one problem," he began giving me a sly, sideways grin.

"And what would that be?" I asked trying to be just as sly but failing as another series of giggles escaped.

"Well, if I win, then that means we'll be stuck in here for the rest of our lives. When do I start collecting on these dates? I mean, you said we'll get out of here someday. That could mean that we escape the day before we die. I think we should set an amount of time for this bet." He argued logically like an experienced debater.

"Well, how about this. You collect on the dates beginning whenever you would like. Today, tomorrow, whenever. And you stop collecting on the dates when we escape." I bit my lip, afraid that we actually would escape, and then he would take the bet seriously and stop seeing me.

"But what if I don't want to stop taking you on dates?" he asked, reading my mind.

"Well, we'll have to work it out then now, won't we?" I was relieved that we both seemed to be on the same page.

"I suppose . . ." was all he said, leaving it open for interpretation.

"So what's your embarrassing story?"

Not only did I want to change the subject, but my curiosity had been nagging at me ever since he had entered the room. I wondered what embarrassing moment could've possibly happened to David. He seemed so cool and collected.

"Well, when I was twenty-two, Leslie joined us." His smile was bitter sweet as he traveled back into the past. "Anyways she gave me this backpack that she found in her room. It was torn and frayed but it had all the planets on it and I used it to carry the books that I found around the house into my room." He looked up at me as if waiting for judgment.

"That's not that embarrassing. Are you saying you were a dork? I had two bookshelves full of books in my room back home."

"Oh, it gets better," he promised. "One day, I hit the jackpot of books when I was exploring downstairs. Instead of going straight to my room, I went to the kitchen first, hungry for a snack. I put the backpack down on the floor and turned my attention to one of Leslie's famous chocolate chip cookies. While I was eating, Jane and Leslie joined me in the kitchen for lunch. They were still eating by the time I left." He smiled at me.

"Anyways, I picked up the backpack before I got up, off the bench. I put the backpack on my back but it was so heavy that it pulled me back and I fell onto the floor." He began laughing as he finished his story. His laughter was infectious, and I began to laugh as I imagined him being pulled off the bench by a backpack. Soon we were both gasping for breath and trying to one up each other with embarrassing stories.

David

I left Ally's room that night, regretting the decision to leave as soon as the door clicked shut behind me. I tried to get a hold of myself as I walked down the hallways. After five years of endless monotony and following the Rules, I was beginning to feel like I wasn't really a person anymore. I even questioned my true feelings and motives behind getting close to Ally. I had no idea how to distinguish between the real and the artificial. I even found myself using some of the same lines I had used on the other girls, and I hated myself more each time I did it.

I couldn't say that I would march right back into Ally's room and tell her everything. I had a lot of decisions to make, and my moral compass had been skewed. It was like I was stuck in a giant magnet, and the arrow pointed the way everyone else told me that it should. My feet automatically led me to Jane's room as it had on so many other nights. I looked behind my shoulder, paranoid that Ally would follow me.

I turned the corner into the last hallway before the kitchen, taking a deep breath as I approached the door across the hall from mine—Jane's door. I knocked three times, wishing that maybe she wouldn't be there. I was stuck needing to be with her, but at the same time, desperately needing to get away. My thoughts took me back to Ally as I waited, picturing her smile. She was open and trusting when we had only been acquainted for just two short days. With her, I couldn't see the cold calculations that I found every time I looked into the other's eyes with the exception of Sam and Leslie.

Finally, Jane cracked the door open, peeking out and then throwing the door wide open and dragging me in like a ravenous wolf.

"I knew you would come around," she announced excitedly.

"I wouldn't go that far."

"It's different this time, I can feel it," she announced happily.

"Maybe," I conceded, wondering if the only reason she noticed a difference was because of my conflicted emotions—probably a by-product of some new method that *they* were developing.

"Maybe!" she yelled, pulling me closer to her.

"Don't you ever get tired of this?" I asked, unable to help myself.

"Sorry, David, some of us don't have the luxury to just pick up and leave," she snapped, tears building in her eyes.

"Please don't cry," I sighed, gathering her up in my arms.

"I do get tired of this," she sniffled. "I get so tired of watching you play the lovesick lapdog." She looked up at me expectantly.

That was the part where I always said, "*It doesn't mean anything though. You know that.*" For once, I wasn't so sure though.

"David?" she asked, snapping me back to attention. "What's wrong?" she asked, slowly stepping back from me.

"Did John tell you if they changed anything this time?" I asked, feeling dangerously close to betraying my wavering emotions.

"He doesn't tell me anything anymore," she pouted, crossing her arms and plopping down on the bed, looking like a toddler. Unfortunately that was just the behavior that made me go to her in an attempt to comfort her.

"Just take this one slowly, okay?" I asked, wrapping my arm around her waist.

"So you do have a feeling about this one!" she shouted excitedly.

"I told you I don't know yet," I insisted, afraid of the consequences an affirmative response would have for Ally.

"Please stay with me tonight," she begged, pleading with her eyes.

"You know that I can't." I took my arm away from her, giving her a quick kiss on the forehead.

I left the room without looking back, already hearing the quiet sniffles that would likely break out into sobs when I left the room. No matter which way I turned, I felt guilt pushing down on me, weighing down each step I took. It was a miracle that the desperate need to stay one minute but abandon the next didn't keep me glued to a spot somewhere in between. I guess that I was always fluctuating between staying and going though.

Ally

"Should I be worried about Jane?" I asked David the next day after he picked me up from my room.

"Hey, you're safe now," David soothed as he took my hand. "She won't hurt you again," he promised, giving my hand a squeeze.

"Yeah," I agreed, beginning to feel awkward in our handhold.

"What shall we do next, m'lady?" His eyes began to sparkle again, and I was glad to see some spark of hope left, even if it wasn't hope for an escape.

"Haven't you wondered how all of this stuff got in here?" I asked, taking my hand back. I refused to just accept to continue living there in complete ignorance.

"I don't know," he answered, evading my questioning.

"So why do you think we're in here?" I asked, trying to think of a logical answer. Maybe I had gotten into a car accident and was in some crazy coma dream. Maybe I was still in the backseat of the car, and what seemed like days was actually hours. Maybe someone was just messing with us.

"I don't know," he repeated as he gave me a pained look. "Maybe we're in hell." He commented quietly.

"I can't imagine that you did anything to land you in hell." I kept my voice soft but firm. On the one hand, I wanted to comfort him, but on the other, I wanted to prove him wrong and call him out on thinking such ridiculous thoughts.

"Well, why do you think we're here?" David turned the question back on me.

"Honestly, I would like to believe this is all some sick practical joke. I really have no idea." I shrugged my shoulders as my mind whirled around the possibilities.

"We're stuck in a place that tortures us and won't let us leave. That sounds a lot like hell to me." He cut in on my thoughts.

I let it go, trying to imagine what I could've done to land me a spot. I shook my head, as I continued to think. Wasn't hell supposed to be all fire and brimstone? I knew that some people believed that there were different circles of hell depending on what offense one committed, but somehow, the house didn't come off as a place of torture to me. Maybe I just hadn't been there long enough to understand what David and the others had gone through.

Ally

The next few weeks passed in a blur as one day blended into the next. I still hadn't met the other two mysterious tenants, Leslie and Sam. David told me that they mostly kept to themselves down the hallway that I still wasn't allowed to explore. They were also on a different schedule than everyone else. John checked out my ribs and reported that I was fit for exercise.

Jane mostly cast me moody glances or ignored me, making my resolution to avoid her way easier than I'd imagined. Michelle continued to give me her absolute kindness and understanding, and I even managed to ask Eric about his tattoos. Michelle actually gave them to him after they had entered the house. I couldn't imagine Michelle giving anyone a single tattoo, let alone a whole sleeve of them.

The most treasured and exciting moments were those that I spent late at night—or at least what felt like late at night—talking to David. He had actually moved into the guest room after forcing me to confide in him that I was still slightly afraid of the dark. That along with the fact that I walked in my sleep gave him all the reason he needed. He was convinced that one night, I would wander out of the room and be crushed by the light, burned by the sun, or caught in any of the other delightful traps that awaited me.

Although everyone had started to talk about the motives behind David moving in with me, absolutely nothing happened. The initial attraction that I had felt toward David developed into more of a friendship. I was not embarrassed or self-conscious at all each night as I fell asleep, most of the time midway through our conversation. Having a guy as a best friend was definitely a change. It was surprisingly comfortable though; I had always gotten along with guys better than with girls.

So I was kind of shell-shocked one night when David walked into the room and voiced a request. He walked in, looking like he was preparing to punch me in the gut, or if we were little kids, maybe steal my Barbie. He sat down next to me and uttered the last words I ever expected to hear from him.

"Ally, I need you to do me a favor." David had started as he walked into the room. My heart sped up as he got closer. I thought it was funny that in such a small amount of time my relationship with David had morphed into such a strong friendship. Although, I was still freaked out because David would sometimes look at me like he thought of me as more than just a friend.

"Sure," I answered automatically. I doubted he would ask anything from me that I wasn't willing to give.

"I need you to try to leave."

"Oh." That was all that I could say. Not caring that my mouth was probably hanging open, I continued to stare at the man that I had come to care for more than any other guy I knew. Did that mean that he didn't care for me like he had led me to believe? Maybe I had just imagined all of those so-called hints and clues that I thought he had been leaving. Suddenly I felt more like a girlfriend being dumped than a friend.

"I thought you said no one could leave," I started, trying to keep the stupid tears I could feel welling up in my eyes from escaping. I was going to have to leave soon. If one thing was certain, I knew I couldn't stand crying in front of David. I never could let myself cry in front of other people. I would either wait until I was out of sight or push back the feelings until later that night when I could weep openly.

"Everyone that has tried to leave ended up right back inside," he confirmed, his face pulled into a tight mask that I couldn't recognize.

"So what use would me trying to leave possibly have?" I asked breathlessly, hoping that he would not tell me he didn't want me after all, that he couldn't stand to live with me there.

"I just think that if you could leave, life would be better," he explained, never breaking eye contact.

"Fine, I'll try to leave right now." I could feel my resolve to keep the tears in breaking as my face began to crumple, probably looking very unattractive. "Let's hope I succeed. I wouldn't want to make life worse for anyone." As I continued to talk, I turned my back and began walking out of the room. I had failed to keep the despair from my face, but I would not show tears.

"Ally, please don't cry." Of course David would know that I was going to cry. He knew me too well. He just didn't want to know me. He put his hand to my face, brushing away the tears that were beginning to flow.

"Good-bye, David," I said, trying to keep my voice from cracking. One way or another, I was going to leave. I would try walking out. And if that didn't work I would just let myself go to one of the many horrifying, and suddenly welcome, surprises. If I couldn't live there, where could I live at that point? Then I shook my head at my stupidity. I would never kill myself for any guy.

I ran out of the room before he could say anything else. As I rounded the corner of the hallway into the main room, making a point to avoid the falling icicle-shaped light—I still wasn't used to the house enough for that action to be a habit—the tears poured from my eyes forming tiny waterfalls that I melodramatically believed would never end. I didn't even care that my nose was beginning to clog up with snot. After experiencing rejection from a trusted friend, the thought of looking unattractive wasn't even near the middle of my list.

I descended the stairs, seeing everything in a blurry haze. I kept my hand on the railing. The last thing I needed was to fall down the stairs and land in the middle of the intricate sun painted on the floor. The idea of suicide may have popped up in the back of my brain as an alternative solution, but I was not one of those people that got caught up in the middle of a depressing situation and immediately jumped to killing myself. I would never do that to my family, even if they did drive me insane sometimes.

I reached the door and stood there debating whether or not I should actually leave. I should've pressed David for more information but trying not to cry in front of David along with my feelings of betrayal diminished my common sense. I turned around, deciding that I wasn't quite ready to leave just yet.

"You really should've kept walking," Jane spat, shaking her head. "That would've been the better alternative," she continued, confusing me as her and the others did so often.

I looked up to see Jane running her hand along the mahogany railing of the staircase. She kept her eyes trained on me, giving me the uneasy feeling of a mouse being stalked by a cat. She slowly walked down the staircase, each step echoing throughout the main room like the slow cadence of a bass drum.

"I wouldn't have come here if you hadn't screamed," I reminded her. "Besides, I would like nothing more than to leave this place right now."

She faltered in her slow, easy movements that had seemed so predatory just moments before. A look of doubt and then pain crossed her face, and I could see some kind of internal struggle as the two emotions interchanged between each other on her face.

"Still," she said, with the look of cruelty and hatred glued back on her face. "We've all experienced the pain of death. You're not that special. I think it's time that someone initiates you."

I knew that I needed to get as far away from Jane as possible. I understood that women could get a little jealous and territorial when the man they wanted was with someone else, but she was just beyond crazy.

"I know that you want David for yourself," I prompted. "But curse or no curse, or whatever the hell is up with this place, you're not a murderer. Besides, he wants me gone just as much as you do."

"But that's just the point. I could slice you up right now, and you would come right back. Sure, you'd feel a little bit of pain for a minute or two but you'd come back. I don't care if you think David finds Richard Simmons more attractive than you. This is for me."

"What is wrong with you?" I asked vehemently.

"It's high time that someone showed you that even you aren't immune to this horrible place. Like I said, you aren't special. Plus, I'll get great satisfaction at watching you suffer." She continued to rant, completely ignoring me.

As I searched my mind for something to say, the only conclusion I could come to was to leave. Maybe I could have dashed for the door and left just as David had suggested. But while I had been backing up slowly to get away, I hadn't realized that she had already been so close. I seriously needed to stop over thinking things.

With blinding speed, Jane slid a kitchen knife into my stomach. The blade was so sharp that it pierced my skin like butter. I only had time to gasp, and then I was on the floor in agony.

"That ought to do it," she said way too cheerily, pulling the knife out. "Now, would you like me to speed it up, or would you rather lie there and suffer a little bit? Suffer, you say? Okay, I'll see you when you get back!" She wiped the blade on her shirt and just watched.

I don't know how long I laid there on the floor. It could've been minutes or hours. The excruciating pain was the only thing I could think of. I could barely remember feeling happy or healthy. After an indefinite amount of time, I began to feel a numb sensation spreading throughout my limbs, almost as if they were falling asleep. I actually started feeling better, mostly because I couldn't feel anything. That was probably a bad thing. I thought I remembered someone on some medical show say to worry when it didn't hurt anymore.

"At least we found someone that he seems to be attracted to," Jane muttered, leaving me at the bottom of the stairs. Her words reached me, but I couldn't interpret their meaning. I thought they might have made more sense if I hadn't lost so much blood. I couldn't understand anything anymore.

As I was slipping into a peaceful unconsciousness and overanalyzing the situation yet again, I was rudely interrupted by someone shaking me. Couldn't anyone just let a girl die in peace?

"Ally? Ally! Wake up!"

"I'm 'wake, you id-yut," I mumbled, mostly incoherent.

"Okay, okay. Oh, God. Please just stay with me, okay?"

"'Kay," I replied, unsure of what I was agreeing to.

That was when I started to feel less numb and tingly and more agonizing pain. There was something pushing on my stomach. I tried to push the pressure away but my hands flopped back down beside my body like fish out of water. I tried to look up at David, but even my head was weighed down to the ground.

"Just stay still, okay?" David pleaded. He shouldn't have been so worried. It would all be over soon. It wasn't right for him to be scared.

" 'Kay," I promised trying to make him calm down.

And then I was floating in the air. If not for the terrible pain, dying would be pretty cool. Of course, if I wasn't so delirious I would've realized that David was carrying me up the stairs. The next thing I knew, I was lying in the bed that I had woken up in just three weeks before.

"S'not so bad." I had my eyes closed so I really had no idea if I was actually talking to anyone. I think I was trying to convince myself more than anyone else.

"I'm so sorry, Ally," David pleaded. I couldn't understand why he was so upset. He wanted me gone. And even if he was experiencing second thoughts, he believed I was just going to magically reappear at the base of the stairs.

But I was pretty pissed at Jane. Maybe that was it. Maybe he was sorry Jane had hurt me. Did he even know that Jane was the one that stabbed me? Whatever, it wasn't like he thought there was a funeral in order.

"Why are you sorry? You din't do it. S'not so bad."

Suddenly I felt like someone was ripping my stomach open. I screamed, clenching my hands into fists. I looked up, finally in control of my head and saw that David had peeled his soaked through shirt off my stomach. I caught a glimpse of the four inch-long gash running a diagonal line along the side of my stomach. As soon as David's shirt was gone, the gash immediately began filling with blood with alarming speed. The blood, with nowhere else to go, spilled over the sides of the wound and onto the bed.

"Oh, no," I spoke slowly. My lips felt numb and the blissful calm that came from going into shock was gone. He had brought me back to reality, and he was making me feel the pain. As I moved my gaze from my stomach, I noticed that I had a red-colored tube sticking out from the crook of my elbow. I followed the length of the tube as it circled around and around all the way to David, who was sitting beside me. David was giving me his blood!

John, appearing out of nowhere, pulled a first aid kit out which still just didn't make any sense. I knew my reasoning skills were severely compromised, but in a house where people died and just came back, doctors and medicine seemed obsolete. Maybe it killed John to see people suffer, but when someone was as critically wounded as I was everyone was just supposed to accept the fact that he or she was going to die. It wasn't like they thought I would be gone for long.

Then I thought, completely forgetting about the realization that David was a walking blood bank at that point, maybe John was just going to give me some morphine to ease my suffering.

"It's really not s'bad anymore, don't waste painkillers on me." My slurring was getting worse and with each heartbeat, a brand new stabbing pain pulsed throughout my torso. But still, I couldn't stand them wasting any type of medication on me, instead of using it on a less critical case that wouldn't end in death. I didn't know how regular injuries worked, but everyone kept telling me that when people died, they kind of reset, like characters in a video game respawn.

John looked at me trying to decide what to say. "Shhh, it's ok. It's not a waste. We need to take a look at your wound." John explained trying to sound soothing.

"You're out of practice, doc." I laughed feebly. "Although you get an A for effort, you still sound just as worried as David looks."

"Don't be ridiculous, Ally. You're going to be fine." David interjected, cutting off whatever John was about to say.

"Why? Why are you doing this?" I demanded.

And then another wave of excruciating pain ripped through my stomach as John applied more pressure and then took David over to the corner.

"She has a point. We shouldn't be doing this," John whispered.

"She just can't die, John!" David yelled.

"But she'll come right back. What's the point in drawing out her suffering?" John countered. I had to agree with the guy, but at the same time, I wished they would just make up their minds.

"And here I thought you were a doctor," David insisted.

"That's beside the point! We all come back. I'm not needed here." He was backing out.

"She's special, okay," David mumbled, looking down on the floor.

"How so?" John glanced over at me incredulously.

"I'm sorry, David," John said, backing out of the room. "This is how it has to be."

Even though I had acted so brave before, I let out a sob. I felt abandoned and the fear of dying was suddenly very present and real again.

"Shhh, it's okay," David soothed, sitting beside me. He had removed the tube that was giving me his blood when he left to talk to John, and he didn't bother putting it back in. Without John, there was no hope.

"I'm scared," I said truthfully for the first time.

"Me too," he whispered, stroking my hair.

"Will you stay with me?" I asked, remembering the night I had asked him to do the same. Only then he had been able to save me.

"Of course," he answered instantly.

"Will you kiss me?" I asked, even quieter.

He touched my face, a look of indecision becoming more apparent with each second that he didn't respond.

"It's okay if you don't want to," I supplied, feeling sorry for myself.

Before I could say anything else he bent over, touching his lips lightly to mine. For one instant, a feeling of warmth and happiness replaced the cold fear and pain, and I drifted into a deep welcoming sleep.

David

As much as it had hurt to tell Ally that I wanted her to leave, it hurt even more to see her in pain. Had she even managed an attempt at walking out the front door before Jane had attacked her? Sure, she hadn't implicated Jane as the one that stabbed her, but I wasn't a fool. I could think of no one in the house, including Ally, that would do that other than Jane. If I hadn't just given Ally a dangerously high amount of my blood, I would have tracked Jane down right then. At that point, I wouldn't even have been averse to breaking the "no-hitting-girls rule."

Scratch that. Maybe the reason I couldn't leave Ally's side wasn't that I had given so much blood, but that I was so worried about her that I constantly kept glancing at her face and rising chest to make sure that she was still alive. I couldn't find the will to leave the room. I had promised myself that first day that I wouldn't let anything hurt her, and what did I do? I pushed her away, telling her that she needed to leave, which ultimately put her in a vulnerable position, with no one by her but Jane. I knew I should've followed her when she left the room, barely able to contain her tears.

Michelle and John barged into the room, surprising me. I wiped the look of loss off my face, knowing the knowledge of my true feeling for Ally would be dangerous in anyone's hands.

"You are to do everything in your power to save her," Michelle ordered, leaving John to do his job. She took one last glance at me and left without a word.

"What happened?" I asked, instantly curious. Whatever they knew, I had to know.

"Michelle wouldn't tell me," he answered, getting to work.

John removed the second shirt I had placed on Ally and cut away the rest of her shirt. She still had a bruise on her chest from Jane's first attempt.

"What can I do?" I asked, getting ready to give Ally more of my blood.

"Not that," he answered. "You've already given too much."

"You've forgotten the perks of this house," I reminded him. "So what if I die?" I asked, still getting ready to put the needle back in my arm.

"Fine," he snapped, grabbing the needle and my arm. "You need to think about what you're doing," he reminded me.

He didn't wait for a response before he got back to work. He disinfected the area, and I made a point to look at Ally's face instead of her stomach. I had begun to feel queasy, and it wasn't just the loss of blood. I touched my fingers to my lips again, feeling utterly lost but amazingly alive.

David

John had pulled a cot next to the bed, allowing me to stay in the room with Ally. John's first priority though was for me to rest and recover from my hefty donation. After making me eat a few cookies, drink a glass of orange juice—just like a real donation to the American Red Cross—and extracting my promise that I would get some sleep, he finally left me alone. I began to mull over the events of the night.

John was always a believer that if someone was dying, we should just let her die because drawing it out was just about the worst punishment he could think of. And yet as soon as Michelle had burst into the room, he had consented to give his help. Of course, we already knew that I was the same blood type as Ally, but I wondered what changed that had prompted Michelle to order John into action.

Maybe she just couldn't let go of that need to help the victims of injuries. If I stopped trying to delude myself though, her action came directly from them. It was all part of the large picture—part of the cause. Whatever the case, John seemed to side with me in my conviction that we shouldn't let Ally die. Weird.

Mostly I was just relieved that I could help, especially because I knew that Ally had been very close to losing about four, definitely fatal pints of blood. Still, it seemed that he was almost too keen on helping. Sure, he had asked why we were saving Ally, but John had always been a terrible actor. I just couldn't shake the feeling that he was hiding something from me. Maybe he was finally starting to believe that Ally was different. But what had Michelle said to bring him around to my way of thinking?

All my thoughts made up a jumbled mess inside my brain and that, combined with the loss of blood, made my head feel like a ton of lead. Soon I found myself leaning my head on the big, king-sized bed despite my efforts at fighting my fatigue. Finally, I gave in and made the unconscious decision to rest my head and let my mind wander. Usually, when I just relaxed and let my mind take me where it wanted to go, I came to my best conclusions. My head hit the pillow, and no idle musings made their way into my thoughts as blackness enveloped me.

Ally

I was in a bed. But the bed felt stiff, almost like a gurney. There were men standing around me that I hadn't met before. I couldn't make anything else out other than their faces and the white doctor coats that they were wearing. Had some new people entered the house? Maybe one of them was Sam. What was up with their clothes? I would have to warn them about all of the traps spread throughout the house like land mines. I tried to talk to them, but I couldn't seem to find my voice.

They were whispering to each other, but I couldn't make out any of the words. They looked worried. I was sure I had looked like that the first day I entered the house. And then they started touching my stomach.

"Who are you? John never introduced me to you. Are you new?" I mumbled with a dry, raspy voice. Still, they just kept touching me. It was like they hadn't even heard me speak. I couldn't get up. I wanted to run away, or at least to see what those odd men were trying to do.

"Don't touch me. Stop, you're hurting me!" I gasped. Even though I was pretty sure I had yelled at them, the men didn't look fazed at all. One of the men produced a syringe, adjusting an overhead light. The light fell on my eyes for only a second, but I was temporarily blinded, a burning ball of light caught in my vision each time I blinked.

According to my track record, I should've passed out by then, but I couldn't leave. As I struggled with the restraints, pleading with the men to give me a sedative (going on completely unheard), I began to hear voices in my head.

"How's she doing, David?"

"She definitely has a fever. She's delirious. She's been ranting and raving about new people. She might have an infection."

"All we can do now is to keep an eye on her."

"Do you think she'll be okay?"

"It's hard to say. If she gets past these next couple of days, she has a chance, but we need to get her temperature to a safer level. You know this might prove pointless, right?"

"It's not pointless."

"Yeah, that's what I keep hearing"

"I can just feel it."

"Is this a feeling you're getting for the situation or a feeling you have for her?"

"Please just trust me. I think that she could get us out of here."

"Impossible!"

"Well, obviously Michelle agrees with me."

"Michelle has her own reasons for doing this, reasons that you know can't get everyone out of here."

Great, I really was going crazy.

David

John had come into the room right after Ally had stopped screaming. I was sleeping peacefully. There were no dreams, no problems, no worries; just blissful darkness surrounded me. I hadn't even realized my head had fallen onto Ally's arm. That is, I hadn't realized it until Ally began to thrash around as if a hive of bees was attacking her. I jumped up, scanning the room for any sign of trouble, half expecting to see Jane standing in the corner preparing to finish the job with her kitchen knife.

Then Ally started screaming, telling people to get away from her, that they were hurting her. I tried to hold her hands down to keep her from tearing the stitches open that John had so carefully placed. If no infection set in, Ally would live. She would be left with a nasty scar and weeks of pain and careful movements, but she wouldn't die. It was miraculous. If John wasn't so stubborn and annoying one moment and then completely willing the next, I would've hugged him. They were up to something.

Finally, Ally relaxed and only mumbled a few incoherent sentences before settling back into a light, restless sleep. That was when John came in and actually seemed concerned for Ally.

"Is everything okay?" he asked, searching the room. He was probably looking for Jane just as I had done.

"Yeah she was just having a nightmare," I explained nonchalantly. Sleep talking was a common occurrence when sleeping in the same room as Ally. She had had a few nightmares but none as intense as that one. Still, I blew it off as just another dream.

"Did she open up any of her stitches?" he asked, walking toward the bed and checking her stomach, not even bothering to wait for my answer.

"Anyways, I brought you some dinner. I finally managed to make some spaghetti without some unseen disaster destroying the meal." He offered me a plateful of spaghetti and a glass of milk, and I took it, my mouth watering at the delicious aroma of his special tomato sauce. I snatched a fork and began to shovel noodles into my mouth, not caring that individual noodles were hanging from my mouth. I probably looked like a pig, but the only person I was trying to impress was basically in a coma, and my stomach growled noisily, demanding more.

The only sound that betrayed John as he left the room was the click of the door. I placed my plate on the nightstand next to the big, plush bed and chugged down the rest of my milk. I placed the glass by the plate and stretched, being careful with my right arm; it was still sore from my donation. Finally I could think with a clear head as I leaned against the bed watching Ally. She must've been having an upsetting dream because her eyebrows were furrowed, and her nose and mouth were scrunched up into the cutest scowl I'd ever seen. I couldn't imagine Ally as intimidating.

I wanted to wake her up and release her from her troubling dream, but the rest seemed more important. I didn't even know if I could wake her up at that point. I was going to have to have a very long talk with Jane.

Ally started mumbling again and I turned my attention back to her, watching her expressions change. Not only did I want to get to know Ally better, but it began to feel imperative to keep her alive. I just didn't want to seem too pushy or stalkerlike. Again I resolved to be more honest with her, and again I struggled with the weight of my decision.

Thinking about the possibility that Ally could actually wake up, I decided to rest my head and sink back into the cot before she opened her eyes and saw me staring at her. That would definitely result in a creeper vibe, the one thing that couldn't happen. She would start to avoid me, leaving her wide open to danger. I didn't even realize I was drifting off as I continued to contemplate the best possible options to keep Ally safe.

Ally

When I finally regained consciousness again I opened my eyes slowly, afraid that I would still find a group of men in white lab coats around me. Instead I found myself in John's bed. I felt like I was beginning to lose my mind. I had made a habit of getting into trouble and waking up in John's bed. That fact didn't bother me. The strange, lifelike dreams did.

I pulled down the blankets, afraid of what I would find but unable to stop myself. I needed to see the damage that Jane had done. I pulled the blankets down easily enough but I hesitated before lifting up my shirt. I had expected to find my shirt cut away with maybe a little bit of gauze covering the wound but someone had wrapped a bandage around my waist a few times. I reached to lift up the fabric but as I flexed my stomach a sharp stab of pain took me by surprised, and I let out a small gasp.

A gash about three inches long puckered out around the edges of at least thirty stitches. An angry red color began in the middle and reached outward toward the rest of my stomach. I snapped my bandage back down hastily and accidentally bumped the end of the stitches, causing another sharp stab. I tried to push down the tears, imagining falling on the ground when I was a child. I would cry for a moment but then I would stand up again, tearing off again at a run. Although I had earned the nickname lumpy for all the bumps and bruises, my father had also called me a trooper—both nicknames I was proud of.

The gash scared me, and even though I had come to be proud of all my scars, that one was just too much for me to handle. A huge scar that would grab everyone's attention—even though they would act like they weren't staring, only to occasionally glance at it when they thought I wasn't looking—already made me feel self-conscious.

I lifted the stretch fabric up again, determined to accept the new scar as a part of me. That didn't mean I had to accept the person that had done it though. I imagined taking out my revenge on Jane, but no matter what scenario I played out in my head, I knew I would never be able to bring myself to inflict any physical harm greater than a slap in the face.

I contemplated getting up and finding David or John, but instantly dismissed the idea when even a small flex of my abdominal muscles tore through my stomach like someone was grabbing my intestines and twisting them.

"Well, at least cramps won't ever feel that bad again," I laughed to myself, and then mentally added it to my not-to-do list.

Instead of a things-to-do list, I had a things-not-to-do list. No getting up, no laughter, basically no movement whatsoever. I wondered how much time it took for a stab wound to heal. Sure it took about a week or two for a small cut to heal, but I couldn't make myself think about all the layers of skin and muscle and maybe even organs that Jane had destroyed. What a bitch.

The doorknob began to twist as I continued to think of a whole butt ton of bad words to call Jane. My heartbeat accelerated, wondering whether or not anyone had an eye on Jane. Maybe she was standing outside the door, gleefully wielding another weapon from the kitchen. Hopefully everyone was smart enough to let her think that she had succeeded the first time.

Well, actually the second time since I assumed that her suggestion that I take a shower was definitely an attempt on my life. I sincerely hoped that the old saying "third time's the charm" was just that—an old outdated cliché that had no bearing whatsoever.

I let out a breath of relief when I saw David sneak through the door and close it just as softly as he had opened it.

"Hey," I greeted him, a huge smile spreading across my face.

"Hey," he said, some of the worry fading from his eyes. "We gotta be quiet," he added, looking at the door.

"I'm supposed to be sleeping in my room and leaving you some peace and quiet so you can sleep off your injury. You've been out for two days," he looked down at my stomach, sucking in a deep breath.

"Oh," I looked down, forgetting that I hadn't pulled my shirt back down after the last inspection.

"It's really not that bad," I lied and then started laughing at my ridiculous attempt to downplay my injury.

"Okay, maybe it's that bad," I agreed, wincing at the pain and gasping for breath.

"Are you okay?" he asked seriously.

"I'm alive," I said, grabbing his hand. "I'm alive, but not respawned or whatever," I added, holding his hand tighter as he tried to pull it away.

"Why is that?" I asked looking up at him.

"John changed his mind," he shrugged, sitting down next to me.

"I'm sorry, Ally," David apologized for the hundredth time. "You were leaving because of me. You were alone because of me." He shook his head, once again blaming himself for every single little thing that happened to me.

"Sooner or later, Jane would've gotten to me. She didn't know I was trying to leave. She was jealous because she thought I was stealing you away from her." I argued, trying to get through to him.

"Maybe," was all he would say in response, falling into a silent stupor.

I sat there with him silently, wondering what good he planned on doing for me by sitting there sulking. I couldn't understand his eagerness to blame himself for every single mishap.

"Why are you here?" I snapped, surprising him out of his blank, melancholic stare.

"I wanted to check on you," he answered, wide-eyed.

"Well, you checked on me and now, you're just bumming me out. Do you think I want to hear a guy blame himself for someone else hurting me? That's just as frustrating to me as my forgiveness is to you," I shot at him, coming as close to yelling as I could without sending a fresh wave of pain through my stomach.

"But it's my fault," he cried stubbornly, making me want to shake him.

"Okay look, I'll stop forgiving everyone for everything if you stop blaming everyone, including yourself, for everything." I promised, pretty sure that he would shoot down the idea.

"That's ridiculous," he said loudly, also not quite reaching yelling volume.

"Okay, then I'll get up right now, march right up to Jane and say, 'Jane I forgive you for stabbing me in the stomach, I understand where you're coming from.' How does that sound?" I shot back, ready to match him word for word in stubbornness.

"Now hold on just a minute," he grabbed my hand quickly as if I really had the ability to even get out of bed.

"I can't help the way I feel," he started, holding up his hand when I opened my mouth to cut him off. "But I'll stop criticizing you for the way you feel," he promised.

"Easier said than done," I pointed out.

"Well, as long as you don't plan on forgiving Jane any time soon, I think I can manage."

As he got up, I could tell that he was planning his retreat. It wasn't that he looked like he wanted to leave, but more like he was trying to find the words to do so.

"Going so soon?" I asked, wanting desperately to tell him to stay and keep me company. Not only did I enjoy spending time with him, but he made me feel safe, as if in every moment he was with me absolutely nothing bad could happen. Whether I was afraid of my own imagination or of Jane coming in to finish what she had started, I just couldn't find the words to make him stay.

"It's getting late, and I am under strict rules after all," he responded, leaving me with an empty feeling inside before he even walked out the door.

"Goodnight," was all I could say, closing myself off before he left in the hopes that once he did leave I wouldn't feel his absence quite so much.

" 'Night," he whispered, closing the door behind him.

In the end, my attempt to distance myself actually caused more harm than good. I began to cry in the dark room, justifying my whirlwind of emotions as a product of a traumatic day but throughout the cry-fest, I flipped back and forth between feeling sorry for myself and a total meltdown in which I didn't even know why I was crying anymore.

After I managed to plug up the waterworks, my nose was plugged to the point where I could only breathe out of my mouth. There was not a single Kleenex in the room, and I was faced with the choice of wiping my snotty nose on John's six hundred thread-count sheets or pulling myself up out of bed and trying to make it to the bathroom.

Finally I settled on trying to make it to the bathroom. Even though I had already spilled over a pint of my blood on his bed, I couldn't bring myself to blowing my nose into his pillow case. I already knew that sitting straight up would be a bad idea, seeing as that would require me to flex my abdominal muscles. I literally felt glued to the bed even though there was absolutely nothing holding me down.

I shuffled my body toward the edge of the bed and let my legs hang off the side. Next, I rotated my body so that I was lying on my side, figuring that the upward movement most unlike a crunch would be the best plan of action. I pushed myself up with my right arm and found myself upright sooner than I had thought possible. Black dots immediately began to color my vision, reminding me that I hadn't had anything to eat since breakfast, and I was also currently short on blood.

I immediately began to question the intelligence of my plan. Maybe a little bit of snot on top of all that blood wasn't such a bad idea. But right after that thought left my head another one snuck its way in. Anger over my helplessness took over and before I knew it, I was walking toward the bathroom, using the walls as support. Luckily, the bathroom was only about ten feet away from the room.

As soon as I reached the bathroom, I grabbed the Kleenex box and sank down to the floor, beginning to cry again. I swiped at my face angrily as my helplessness bubbled up again. There I was stuck on the bathroom floor with no plan to get back to John's bed and a sinking feeling that I was all alone.

For the first time in months, I found myself wishing for my parents. All I wanted was to wake up on the bathroom floor after having a nightmare to my mother's soothing words.

"Screw it," I said to myself, lying flat on my back on the bathroom floor. The cold tiles felt amazing on my back, and I only wished that I could lie flat on my stomach to get some cold to the burning flesh at the edges of my wound. I tried to block everything from my mind, sinking into a state of calm before finally falling asleep, happy that it was voluntary on that occasion.

Ally

Someone jostled my arm, bringing me out of my stupor. I jumped, causing a fresh wave of pain to course through my entire body. Not only did my stomach ache, but my whole body ached after spending a night on the bathroom floor. I was relieved to see Michelle crouching over me, instead of Jane, or even David at that point.

"How'd you get here, honey?" Michelle asked in a motherly tone, causing a fresh wave of tears to spring from my eyes.

"I wanna go home," I sobbed, completely ignoring her question.

"Shhhh, it's going to be all right," she soothed, brushing the hair off my soaked face.

"Nothing is all right," I yelled. "Is this all right?" I asked, pulling up the bandages on my stomach.

"Most definitely not," she agreed, resting her head against the wall.

"I'm starting to feel like I just need to wake up, and everything will be okay," I joked dryly.

"Wouldn't that be nice." Michelle replied tensely.

"Why do I get the feeling that everyone here knows something that I don't?" I asked, once again frustrated by my complete lack of understanding.

"I don't know which case is worse in this situation," she started haltingly. "Is it better to be in the dark, questioning those around you, or to be questioning yourself about everything you know?" she asked, more to herself than to me.

"I don't know what you people are talking about, but it's starting to freak me out."

I pulled myself up so that I was resting against the wall across the room from Michelle.

"I'm glad you have some spunk. It definitely changes things," she remarked, once again making me feel uncomfortable.

I chose to take that as a compliment, figuring that maybe I brought some spice to their lives. The silence stretched between us as I began to wonder who I could trust in the household. Even Michelle the Therapist was starting to creep me out.

I tried to lift myself up off the floor but couldn't make it past a few inches without that annoying spike of pain.

"Here, let me help you," Michelle offered, holding out her hand.

"Thanks," I said, grabbing her open palm.

Michelle led me to the bedroom, promising that she would bring me some breakfast. I didn't feel like I could eat after a steel blade had interrupted my digestive system, but my stomach disagreed with me. I sat on the bed, feeling empty of not only food but emotion as well.

I fell asleep before Michelle got back, waking up a few hours later to find cold pancakes sitting on the bedside table. I ate them quickly, feeling the comfort of fullness filling me up as I ate. After shoveling the food into my mouth, I sat back in bed and relaxed, drifting off into a peaceful sleep, unconsciously deciding that I would just have to find answers by myself.

Ally

The days and nights would've blurred together in an endless cycle of fear and boredom if it weren't for David. We spent most of every day together, playing truth or dare—even if I was greatly limited in my abilities to perform anything in the dare category. I thought the truth section of the game would allow me to find out the reality behind my situation, but David always found a way to evade my questions. Still, I actually started enjoying our daily routine when John cleared me from bed rest.

John warned me that I would have to pace myself a lot more than I had after my sprained ribs (David had told him that I went swimming), poking and prodding as he spoke. I made a mental checklist drowning out the heap of rules and warnings:

1. Hunt down David the snitch.
2. Make a schedule to avoid Jane.
3. Find out what everyone was keeping from me.
4. Eat as much food as I could find.

Even though staying in bed for what must've been a month doesn't sound that taxing, I hadn't been able to keep much food down because of the painkillers. Oh yeah, and maybe the hole in my stomach didn't help.

I stood up, giving John one last reassurance that I would be good, not really caring whether or not I sounded convincing when my stomach gurgled. I honestly could have eaten the first edible piece of food I saw. I mentally changed my list, making food my first priority with a clause to look out for Jane as I hunted. Sure I was hungry, but I wasn't going to run into Jane and let her set me back a whole extra month in my hastiness to find fatty, salty goodness.

I daydreamed of pizza rolls and orange pop, causing my stomach to let out another loud protest and making John laugh.

"Go on then, get some food," he said, putting a hold on his marathon of a speech.

But David stopped me on my way to the kitchen, changing my list of priorities back to the original order. We stood a few inches apart, an unexpected web of tension stretching between us. What, since I was back on my feet, it was time to act cold and distant?

"Follow me," he said, holding out his hand.

My brain froze, unable to predict where he was taking me. Hunger forgotten, I began to imagine kissing David. I flashed back to the kiss he had given me the night I was supposed to die. I thought of moving my fingers through his hair and pulling him down to my level as I tiptoed to reach his.

But as I got lost in my fantasy land, David was preparing to pull me down to reality.

"You need to try again," he said bluntly, snapping me to attention as we reached the staircase.

"David, you said yourself that no one can leave," I argued desperately, trying to grasp at anything that would keep me close to David. Again, questioning my ability to feel so strongly for someone in just a few short months, especially when I knew he wasn't being completely honest with me. I imagined people like my mother shaking their heads at my naïve belief that I could trust David.

"I said everyone that has tried to leave ended up back inside, but you haven't tried," he persisted, repeating his previous argument.

"Okay, fine," I snapped, grabbing my hand away and marching down the stairs. "And a happy recovery to me," I muttered, resenting him for getting my hopes up with the promise of a surprise, only to ask me to leave.

I walked to the door without saying good-bye, both too angry and too hopeful to speak—angry at David and hopeful that I would see him again in just a few short seconds.

I looked back to see David at the top of the staircase watching me with an odd look. I saw hope in his eyes, and while I was hurt that he actually wanted me to succeed in leaving, I understood that he probably just wanted me safe. Still, the irrational side of me wished that he would stop me, tell me that he couldn't live without me. All that mushy crap that had seen on television that would make me want to gag. Maybe it was just the bad acting, or maybe I didn't understand the feeling until that moment.

Even though it hurt that he wanted me to leave, it still didn't hurt as much as the first time that he asked me to try it, not taking into account the fact that I was stabbed in the stomach by Jane. I understood that even though he wanted me to leave, David still felt the same hurt that I did. He probably felt worse, being trapped in that hell hole.

Finally I turned around, placing my hand on the doorknob, understanding that the night would either end with me out in the cold or unable to leave. Looking back, I should've been prepared for a possible third option. Usually, my constant need to rationalize everything always ended in a few possible scientific explanations, but my time spent there threw rationality out the window every day.

I pushed the door open, gazing out into the night and saw the road right away. My car was still right where I left it, which was odd because someone should've found it by then. I stepped out the door and felt myself falling for what felt like an infinite amount of time. And still I kept falling, waiting to hit the bottom and shatter into a million pieces.

Suddenly I was only aware of black and white dots, almost like the ant races that occur on a television screen when the channel doesn't work. I didn't feel any pain, but I didn't really feel anything at all. I couldn't feel my body, and I wasn't sure I was completely coherent. Sure I was aware that I couldn't feel anything, but that was really the only thought that crossed my mind. I forgot everything that had bothered me, not just within the unknown time span that I had lived in the house, but every problem that had haunted me since childhood. Unfortunately the bliss of being unconscious to pain did not last long.

I was first aware of a constant beeping sound next to my left ear. I kept my eyes closed, first exploring with my ears, then with touch. I heard a low murmur of voices not too far off, maybe in the next room. As I tried to move my hands, I realized that they were secured to the edge of the bed—a realization that caused the consistent, rhythmical beating to pick up speed, simultaneously causing an abrupt halt in conversation.

I heard footsteps closing in on me, but still I kept my eyes firmly shut, trying to keep them still as if I was sleeping.

"Oh, god, I hope she's not going to start bleeding all over the table again," a male voice sneered, sounding more concerned about the table than a human being.

"You have to admit it's very interesting," a female voice interjected, making me think someone was on my side. Somehow though, the word *interesting* just gave the wrong connotation as I replayed it in my head.

"She may be what we've been searching for," the woman continued, proving my concern to be valid as the uneasiness grew, and the pace of the beeping increased yet again from what I guessed to be a heart monitor.

"Hmm," the woman clicked her tongue nervously, feeling my wrists for a pulse.

"I don't know why you're even worried," said the man, sounding haughtier with each word. "It's not like this is an uncommon occurrence," he added.

"Right, so we should ignore our test subject when she's in possible distress, and maybe next time she gets injured, we'll be oblivious as she bleeds out," the woman snapped.

At least someone was somewhat on my side. But just as interesting had caught my attention, *test subject* was like a red flag, reminding me that I was not a person to them. I was a means to an end—an end that I was oblivious to.

I tried to get my heart rate to decrease, almost on the verge of hyperventilating.

"Maybe this will help," the woman offered.

"Yeah, let's waste more money to make her feel comfortable," he complained.

Suddenly I felt a burning sensation in my arm and, unable to control my reaction, my eyes snapped open as I tried to pull my arm back. The woman dropped the syringe that she had inserted into my IV, staring at me with wide eyes. The man covered his mouth, looking very upset and quite girly. I imagined a girlish squeal coming out of his mouth.

Even though whatever they had given me began to spread warmth throughout my body, it didn't keep me from panicking as I considered all the nasty experiments they would run on me on top of the ones that they had already done.

"Impossible," the woman stuttered, finally finding her voice.

"Apparently not," the man muttered wide-eyed. I couldn't help but notice a slight tinge of contempt, a look that was currently mirrored by my own eyes.

"What does this mean?" the woman asked, checking my pulse nervously. She opened my eyes with her fingers, shining a flashlight into them. I squinted as the light burned my eyes.

"This is going to be fun," he said, speaking more subconsciously than actually answering the woman's question.

"Excuse me?" the woman demanded, snapping him out of his thoughts.

"Imagine the possibilities," he amended, not clearing anything up for me at all.

"Right," she agreed halfheartedly, pulling him into another room where they began actively arguing, hand motions and all.

Since I obviously wasn't going anywhere, I took the opportunity to glance around in an attempt to learn more about the mess I was in. I searched for a company logo or policy. I turned my head to the right, finding David's unconscious body lying on a table identical to mine, arms also strapped in with an IV going into his left arm. One by one, I found everyone from the house lying on a table.

The tables formed a circle around the room which wasn't too odd. Jane's position in the middle of the room caught my attention though, wires hooked up to her and leading to each of us. My hands itched to check for scars, or implants, or God knew what else, but I was held firmly in place by the fuzzy restraints. I wanted to fight against my imprisonment and basically throw a fit, but fighting with an immovable foe such as handcuffs would have made me feel worse. I began to cry at the hopelessness of everything. Apart from advancement in some experiment, I didn't mean anything to anyone anymore.

When the two doctors came back into the room, the woman's eyes were shooting the man with daggers of contempt, but the man only smiled. He was obviously the victor of whatever battle they were fighting.

"Ally, I'd like to ask you some questions *alone*, if that's okay." He stressed the word *alone*, making the woman behind him cross her arms in defiance, obviously not giving up that easily. I mean, weren't captors—like parents—supposed to show a united front with the captive?

"She seems to think that's a bad idea," I pointed out, unwilling to give into anything that easily. Besides, I didn't want to be alone in the same room as a guy that didn't care if I was in pain.

The woman smirked, but quickly hid her smug look under a veil of concern when the man glanced back at her.

"Besides," I added, "you seem to know a lot about me, but I don't even know your name."

"Yes, and it's going to stay that way," the man snapped. "And now, if you would please come with me, I have some questions for you," he said, no longer asking.

The wrist restraints snapped open after he glanced back at what I could only describe as a control room.

"That would've been cooler if you would've snapped your fingers," I joked, wiping the all-powerful glow from his face, a look that came back full force when he smacked me across the face and pulled me off the table, dragging me into a small, dark room. My ears were still ringing when he threw me down and chained me to the floor.

"How did you get out of there?" he asked vaguely.

"Get out of where? You know you should really work on your vague pronoun references," I joked lamely.

"Nerd," he muttered, surprising me.

"You're calling me a nerd? I mean look at you," I shot back, pointedly looking him up and down.

"How did you manage to escape from the house and wake up?" He rephrased his question, over-enunciating each syllable.

"I walked out the front door," I answered bluntly. "That's usually how you leave a house," I added, unable to help myself.

"You think that you're so hilarious. You won't be laughing when this is over," he promised.

"Why do you have it out for me?" I asked. "What did I ever do to you?"

"I thought I was the one asking the questions here," he said, slapping me again.

"I have a family you know. People will be looking for me." I hissed, gritting my teeth while I struggled with the restraints. Who was he to be playing with our minds? Had he never taken an ethics class in his life?

"That little problem, my dear, has been entirely taken care of. We learned the art of cloning quite some time ago."

He laughed at me as if I was some stupid grade school student that knew nothing about the advances in science. But if I was entirely honest with myself, I didn't know the entire extent of those advances.

"Oh yeah, well, what about the scar on my shoulder? It's a pretty nasty scar. I'm sure that they would notice something like that missing."

"We have accounted for every scar," he countered with a smirk tracing his hand down my right temple and along my cheek. I shuddered remembering that he had been in entire control of my body since I had gotten out of the car and walked into the barn, maybe even before.

"Okay, so I get that you have a god complex, but why are you doing this?" I was trying to stall. "And what are you going to do now that I'm awake?"

"Well, we knew that you were different. Every time that you got hurt in your mind, in the simulation, you also physically got hurt. At first, we were astonished. Quite frankly we were afraid. We figured that if you really did die, we would have a dead body on our hands, not that we couldn't have taken care of the evidence. We may tread a thin line between right and wrong, but we're not murderers. Luckily we had someone inside to look after you."

"Oh, so kidnapping isn't completely wrong? Wait, who's working for you inside the house?"

He actually thought he was still straddling the line between right and wrong. I also couldn't help but notice that he had mentioned that *they* weren't murderers, whoever they were. And I felt completely betrayed at the revelation that one of the people I had gotten to know, not counting Jane, was working for them. I doubted Jane worked for them. She was the only one that consistently tried to get me hurt and didn't lift a finger if I was in trouble.

I went cold, thinking that the only person that had constantly been there to help me was David. He couldn't have been working for them though; that was impossible. I felt like I had actually gotten close to him with all our conversations that lasted hours and hours. I hoped to God that he was not just trying to get information from me.

"We're doing a lot of good here. This research has advanced our knowledge of mental illnesses, military conditioning for pain, and so much more. And now that we have you, our research has expanded tenfold. Imagine if the world you see in your mind can actually affect your body, why can't your mind affect the world?"

He ranted on and on. He should've applied some of his research on mental illness to himself.

"Of course this whole program wouldn't be possible if we didn't have two very rich parents paying for a possible cure for their poor daughter." He seemed to be mocking the parents.

"Please don't tell me that I'm in that hell hole to save Jane," I gasped, cutting him off in the middle of his rant. "Are you just going to keep me here in this cell for the rest of my life experimenting on me? If you're going to do that, can you at least tell her to stop being such a psychopath? It is Jane isn't it?"

All those people mind-trapped inside that house were being tortured every single day whether they fell into a trap or not. And if Jane was the one we were there to save, it was time that she got a reality check.

"You're going to do much more than save Jane." He smiled at me, completely ignoring everything that I had said.

"Okay, then. Thanks for all the information. Would it at least be possible for you to point me to the nearest restroom first?" I asked stalling for time. I wanted to find a way to escape from the bathroom. It had worked for that little kid in *The Mummy Returns*, and he had been on a moving train. He got caught about thirty seconds after he escaped, but it was still worth a shot.

"Don't worry, we have plenty of catheters in stock." Okay, eewwww, that was just plain gross. And again he was giving me that nasty, creepy smirk, almost like he had x-ray vision. Sure science was advancing, but I doubted the creep could see through clothes. He probably just snuck peeks while I was unconscious, and I so did not want to go there.

"So am I not even a person to you people?" I was really getting angry at the pompous, arrogant man that dared to call himself a scientist. I could have compared him to Doctor Frankenstein, but at least Doctor Frankenstein only worked with dead people.

"That is an entirely correct assumption." He winked at me, actually winked at me, as he started walking toward me with a giant syringe filled with milky white liquid. "Don't worry, this will hurt a lot less than the pain you've felt since this little experiment began."

"You're an asshole," I spat, shrinking away from the needle. "I'm going to figure out who's working for you inside that house." I crouched back as far as I could before the chains were taut and the metal cuffs were cutting into my wrists. The creep finally reached me, grabbing my neck, and stabbed the needle slowly into my flesh. I yelped in shock, and my face distorted into a mask of pain that he most likely enjoyed. But the puncture wound was nothing compared to the searing pain that raced down my neck as he depressed the plunger.

I was getting really tired of unwilling unconsciousness, especially the weird dreams that came along with it. As I spiraled down the same tunnel as that first night I fell asleep in my car, I once again felt eyes boring into the back of my head. When I turned around though, John was the only person looking at me.

"John! This isn't real we need to get out now," I shouted. But again he stared at me, uncomprehendingly and I thought it had to be a dream. What was going on with my head? I was probably actually in an insane asylum somewhere ranting about people dying and coming back while the doctors shook their heads, and my mother sat there hopelessly wringing her hands together. Yep, I was probably lost to the world.

Then I was back in the house at the base of the stairs, and once again John was waiting for me in the middle of the landing on the second floor. I just stood there looking at him for a few minutes trying to decide the exact clinical term for the illness I was suffering from.

"This can't be real," I whispered under my breath, mostly to myself. "How long have I been gone?" I asked louder, directing my question toward John. I was half expecting him to continue to stand there silently like in my dream. I heard once that the definition of madness is doing the same thing over and over again, expecting different results. I could have walked out that door again, and maybe I would have woken up back in the laboratory or maybe I would have woken up somewhere else. But if leaving once had resulted in me standing back at the base of the stairs, then I wasn't about to prove to myself the full extent of my madness by leaving again and starting right back at the beginning.

"About a day," John answered, watching me like a hawk. "You've been gone the longest out of all of us that have tried to leave." He continued to watch me as if I was a puzzle that he was trying to figure out.

"Hungry?" he asked as he turned around and began walking toward the kitchen. I figured he meant for me to follow, and my stomach went back to the protests it had been making before David asked me to leave for the second time. If that experience with the creep was real, I had been gone for a day without food. I was completely ravenous, and the smell of dinner was like a fishing line, reeling me in.

Ally

As soon as I entered the kitchen, my eyes immediately found David. He looked up, and our eyes locked. First he looked shocked and almost glad to see me again, but as we continued to look at each other, he radiated despair. Was it really so terrible that I was back in his life? So what if I was in trouble from time to time. Every single person living there was in danger. Besides, apparently it was all in their minds. Then I realized that maybe I was the only one that absolutely should not be there as I remembered the creep's revelation that I could actually get hurt.

My mind was *special*, but I didn't feel so special right then. Wasn't I weak because I gave in to the experiences of my mind? Everyone else came back when they died in the house. I was the only one that was so vulnerable that I actually died because of a dream world that mad men had created. Or maybe I could imagine that I was okay and then would be okay. Maybe if I just thought of something happening, then it would happen. I just wanted to eat dinner, forget about my encounter with the crazy man with the comb-over, and spend some time with David because even though I had only known David for a very short time, I trusted him more than anyone else.

Then I remembered that someone in the house, the dream world was a traitor to everyone else living there. My suspect list was incredibly long seeing as everyone in the house always acted in the know. I walked into the room watching David. I trusted him so much; there was no possible way that he could be involved. But he had been there before I stumbled across the threshold. Who knew, maybe I was ambushed while I slept in my car and then walked into the house in my mind. Nothing was certain anymore, but I felt that my trust in David had to be true. My trust in him had to be well placed, or else I really would go crazy.

As I sat next to him, David gave me a huge, rib-cracking bear hug. Even though he forced the breath from me, I still felt not only safe but somehow undeniably right inside his arms and knew that he could not possibly be involved in a huge human rights violation.

After dinner, I asked David to follow me into the guest room. Everyone probably thought we were going to have a monster make-out session—or worse. But whatever they were thinking, they didn't say anything. David eagerly followed me, constantly asking a million questions that revolved around my departure and return. I told him to be patient and that I would talk to him when we were alone, but first I had some questions of my own.

When we walked into the room, I immediately headed toward my bed in the middle and sat down, indicating that David should sit next to me by patting the bed.

"I know we always tend to skip over this subject," I began. "But when did you walk into this mess and how did it happen?"

"I was actually in a hospital after a car accident," he confessed, pulling up the back of his shirt to reveal some wicked scars and burns.

I traced the scars with my fingers, wondering how I missed them when we had gone swimming. For all the moments when I thought that I had been paying attention to everyone else in an attempt to solve the mystery of the house, those scars were something big that I had missed.

I put my hand down abruptly. If I didn't know something that huge about the one person in the house that I had spent almost every waking hour with, I didn't know anything at all.

"I passed out in the hospital and woke up here in John's bed," he finished lamely.

I listened to David's story fascinated by his completely different initiation. I had woken up and then entered the house. I guessed that the doctors injected everyone with serum before they entered the dream house just as Creepy had done to me earlier. Maybe they had gotten to David when he was sleeping in the hospital. Maybe the serum didn't always place a person in the house. Unfortunately, all I had was conjecture. Either way, David's story was surprisingly short.

I needed to talk to John and ask him for his account. I needed to ask everyone for their personal account on their introduction to that life. The knowledge might not help me, but it couldn't hurt. Best case scenario, I could flush out the insider and see if he or she could or would help us all to escape. I wasn't prepared to take no for an answer though.

"David, I need to tell you where I went when I left, and I need you to try to believe me." I glanced at him furtively, not knowing how to start. I felt vulnerable because I needed to open up to David about my experience with the doctors but at the same time I couldn't handle the possibility that he would dismiss my testimony or worse, be on their side.

"Sure, what is it?" He asked keeping his voice light but failing to look prepared for my account.

"I woke up in a hospital bed," I started, not once lowering my gaze from his face in hopes of catching every tiny twitch of emotion. I told him everything, even the part about the creepy doctor who basically implied that he had seen every inch of my body.

He listened and amazingly, kept a reasonable impression of a straight face throughout the whole story. As I finished, he stood up and stared down at me blankly. Gradually, his blank stare turned more thoughtful. He furrowed his eyebrows and unconsciously began to play with the corner of the blanket as he probably went over each sentence again and again.

"I believe you, Ally," he started almost giving me permission to let out a relieved breath. "But what if your experience wasn't real?" He asked, shattering my resolution that we were all trapped in there because of a bunch of doctors with a god complex. "What if it was just a dream? You said yourself that you have extremely vivid dreams in which you can feel pain. You also sleep walk."

"Okay, well then, where did I go? I obviously wasn't here. Are you saying that I got outside, fell asleep and dreamed the whole thing?" I would not be easily persuaded that I had imagined the whole series of events. "For all you know, this could be a dream," I countered.

"That's true I suppose," David conceded. He obviously still had a lot to think over. Heck, I had a lot to think over. I couldn't even make myself believe that I had woken up from some kind of experiment like a lab rat about to lose its brain. If I had indeed shocked the doctors by throwing them the curve ball of my ability to escape from their drug induced sleep how long would it be until they were cutting my brain out and examining it?

Ally

When I told David that I had finally gotten up the nerve to find Sam and Leslie, he insisted on coming along and playing his perpetual role of my bodyguard. I didn't mind though. After all, I hadn't had much luck when I went off on my own, first swallowing about a pint of water and then being stabbed in the gut.

David and I started down the hallway next to the gym entrance. I had never dared to go that way since it was completely forbidden to guests. I figured there must've been nasty surprises every few feet. Oddly enough, the hallway seemed completely safe as David and I walked together, holding hands. His hand completely engulfed mine and I reveled in his warmth.

I began exploring my surroundings. The floor was covered in the same rich burgundy carpet that lined the main hallway and the bedrooms. We had already passed at least eight doors with four on each side mirroring each other. Looking down the hall, I began to believe that we would never reach the end. That the rows of doors would just go on forever.

I glanced up and caught sight of the same iciclelike lights that were hanging from the ceiling in the main hallway. I tightened my grip on David's hand wondering if maybe I had allowed myself to relax too much.

David also looked up guessing my thoughts as I cut the circulation off from his fingers.

"No need to fear, m'lady." He grabbed my arm as if he was my fearless knight, escorting me through perilous land. "These lamps are firmly fixed in place. In fact, nothing in this hallway holds any danger. I know we told you to keep clear, but the real danger comes from the rooms behind these doors."

"Oh," I sighed as I released the breath I had held in for the last minute. "So where do Sam and Leslie live? And why do they live in the most dangerous place in the house?"

"Well, Sam and Leslie live at the very end of the hallway." He paused and stopped walking. "You know, everyone but you and John live down this hall. I used to live here too before I started staying with you. Everyone but Sam and Leslie keeps to the first few rooms though."

"Why didn't you tell me?" I asked, mocking shock and betrayal. "I want to see your old room," I demanded excitedly.

"All right, all right, we're gonna have to backtrack a little though. I lived in the third room on the right."

David held the door open for me insisting that nothing would jump out and decapitate me, eviscerate me, drown me, or kill me in any other unpleasant way that I could think of. David's room shocked me to say the least. I had expected a messy room with clothes haphazardly strewn across the floor and the majority of space occupied by a large, unmade bed.

Instead my gaze fell upon a bookshelf that took up one whole wall filled with books. I noticed that the bottom shelf contained a few anatomy and biology books along with other school textbooks. I had never met anyone that enjoyed reading textbooks during his free time.

"Wow," I breathed, taking in the smell of the thousands, no millions, of pages. My fingers itched to trail over the bindings and snatch a book from its place while my eyes bulged at the endless possibilities that awaited me within those pages.

"I know. You probably think I'm a loser or something." He looked down at the floor, casting me furtive glances with his peripheral vision.

"Definitely not," I laughed, picturing my room back home with piles of books that didn't have a shelf to rest on because I had run out of room. "Let's just say that I share your interest in reading although I don't exactly enjoy reading textbooks during my free time." I looked at the books on the bottom shelf pointedly.

"Yeah, well, I used to dream about practicing medicine, but that dream sort of fell out the window the day I woke up here." Still, David couldn't help but glance at the textbooks, a look of longing in his eyes.

"Hey, if you keep insisting on keeping me alive, then maybe you'll get to turn your dreams into a reality." I didn't realize the meaning behind my words as I spoke them, but they struck a chord within me. I bit my lip—an annoying habit I perform when thinking—and concentrated on my statement. Technically the doctors were turning dreams into reality, or at least a semi-reality. The house wasn't our dream, but it wasn't real life either. It was more like a dream that they had come up with and were forcing us to live through. But the dream held more reality and more consequences for me than for the others.

"You okay?" David asked in a concerned tone. He was looking at me and his right hand moved toward me, but then fell back at his side.

"Yeah I'm fine. I just can't help but think that this actually is a dream that we're somehow living," I admitted.

"I suppose anything's possible," he answered timidly.

"Wow, was that an agreement that I just heard coming out of your mouth?" I asked, not feeling quite so alone anymore.

"Maybe," he answered, neither confirming nor denying in typical David fashion. "Let's go find out answers." He offered me his arm as we left the room.

I was glowing with happiness as David closed the door behind us, a happiness that quickly sputtered out when Jane exited the room directly across from his.

Okay, so it was completely ridiculous to feel jealous of Jane. David had told me about the time the two of them had spent together. He had even confirmed my suspicions—before Jane had stabbed me—that Jane was probably out to get me. He hadn't told me that they had lived right across the hall from each other though.

I clamped down on my ramblings, feeling ridiculous for being jealous of the relationship between my maybe-more-than-friend and his ex-girlfriend. Still, I felt that stubborn pang of the ugly emotion as I watched Jane staring at David. She winked and sent David an air kiss then turned to me and gave me the finger.

"Classy," I remarked, feeling like I needed to get my snub in.

"Says the girl that's shacked up with m'boy, David, here." She looked at David again and actually licked her lips.

"He's not your boy." The anger began welling up inside of me almost boiling over.

"He just doesn't know what he's missing." She shrugged and walked away.

"She's not worth it Ally." I looked at David wondering why he hadn't interjected on his behalf. David returned my gaze pleading with his eyes.

"Why won't you stand up to her?" I demanded.

"It wouldn't do any good," he choked, a shadow passing over his face.

"So what, it is the way it is?" I didn't understand everyone's acceptance of our position.

"I just don't want to start any trouble." His statement possessed certain finality. He wouldn't argue that point with me anymore.

"Okay, well, we better go find Sam and Leslie," I sighed, throwing up my hands in defeat.

We began walking down the hallway in silence. The comfortable companionship that we had shared as we walked down the hall and toured David's room had evaporated. I began counting doors, noticing that each door was constructed of the same dark wood and gold doorknob. By the time we reached the seventeenth set of doors, I finally found my voice again.

"You know I don't blame you for the day Jane attacked me right?" I prompted, getting tired of watching for any change in David's body language or facial features.

"You should," he said simply.

"Why? Because you wanted a better life for me? Because you wanted me out of danger?"

"Don't pretend I didn't hurt you when I told you to leave. I knew I should've gone after you when you left the room. But I just let you go."

"Yes, it hurt to think that you didn't want me, but Jane stabbed me, not you."

"I might as well have." We were both getting frustrated as neither of us would yield to the other's point of view. "You can't change how I feel, Ally. We'll just have to agree to disagree."

"I hate when people say that!" I yelled, crossing my arms and staring David down.

"I hate when the people I love get hurt."

"Like I said, that wasn't your fault. Jane stabbed me and even though you were the one that told me to leave, I hesitated and stood in front of that door for at least five minutes. Wait, people you love?" I registered that David had uttered the *L* word halfway through my rant.

"You love me?" I asked. I expected him to deny his confession or snort while explaining that he meant he loved me like a sister.

"I love you." He repeated his declaration once again throwing me off balance. Did I love him? I had never loved a guy before, so I didn't know the feeling. Sure I was closer to David than I was to anyone else in the world, but I had always thought I only felt friendship or a minor crush. Our behavior toward one another never breached that line between companionship and romance since the night I thought I was dying. Then again, why did I get so jealous when I realized that Jane had lived across the hallway from David?

"Don't feel obligated to say it back." David cut in after a moment of stunned silence and internal debate. "I understand if you don't feel the same way."

Honestly I felt like I had stood up too quickly. I had that light-headedness that was usually accompanied with dehydration or lack of food.

"I love you too," I began. "But right now, I-I just don't know. That love might just come from our friendship." I tried explaining myself in a rush before David could cut me off without knowing the truth.

"Well, we'll just take it slow then." He smiled. "I guess for now though we better get on with the task at hand."

Taking my hand in his, he led me to Sam and Leslie's room.

We reached Sam's room after an eternity of awkward silence. I couldn't stop thinking about David's declaration of love. At first as we continued walking, I took my hand back and kept it tensely at my side, too nervous to hold his hand with the same ease as usual. I accidentally knocked David's hand, not once, not twice, but three times. If I wasn't such a paranoid freak, I really would have believed that David was purposefully putting his hand in the way. The third time we bumped hands together, David grabbed my hand and explained that the third hand bump necessitated handholding.

I laughed hoping that my hands weren't too clammy from my uneasiness. Oddly enough, the friendly and comfortable gesture had changed drastically in the space of mere minutes. The simple touch sent a ripple of excitement up my arm, through my chest, and deep into my stomach. I felt ridiculous and tried to remind myself that I needed to solve the mystery of the mole. I needed to discover the purpose behind our captivity.

David's rapping on Sam's door shocked me out of my reverie. I was unprepared to meet Sam. David had informed me that he was an ex-marine and could probably break my neck with no warning. I could imagine him making me do push-ups for every misstep I took. The fact that he seemed perturbed to see us there did not ease my fears. *So much for a good first impression.* I introduced myself trying not to stare at the floor as I did so. I knew that a salute or whatever other idiotic idea that might pop into my head was a bad plan, so I simply extended my hand for a handshake.

"Hello sir, my name is Ally." I tried to keep my voice even and felt uncomfortable as I tried to hold Sam's gaze. I remembered the first day I met Eric and he had tried to stare me down. Sam had deep blue eyes, the color of the sky on a sunny, cloudless day.

"Sam," he grunted as he grasped my hand and gave it two hard pumps.

"I hope you don't mind, but I just have a few questions about your stay here." As I had predicted, David had stood back to let me acquaint myself. Some people would call his actions rude, but they definitely forced me to speak up. Not that I was comfortable doing so.

"My stay here?" His laughter caused a fit of coughing. Sam reached for a Kleenex and held it up to his mouth, putting his hand up in apology. He tossed the Kleenex into a trashcan across the room.

I finally got a chance to take him in as his distraction allowed my eyes to rove across the features of his face. As I had noticed before, he had deep blue eyes. His hair was completely white, and he had a clean shaven face. I didn't even know any guys that bothered to keep a clean shave. His nose was crooked as if it had been broken, and the wrinkles grooved into his face stretched from his eyes down toward his chin. He must've been at least seventy.

As Sam's coughing finally subsided, he popped a cough drop into his mouth and turned to look at me again.

"What would you like to know, young lady?" he asked conspiratorially. Huh, maybe he wasn't so bad after all.

"How did you get here?" I asked plunging right in. I crossed my fingers as I hoped not to dampen his suddenly good mood.

"I was on my way to some fancy clinic," he explained, his eyes seeing some past moment. "I was diagnosed with emphysema when I was fifty which did nothing to make me kick my smoking habit. Then ten years later, the doc found cancer spreading through my lungs." He paused, and I wanted to offer some kind of condolences but couldn't make myself speak.

"Anyways," he continued, "I drove to Michigan hoping that Beaumont Hospital would be able to help me. I was knocked out for a biopsy. I woke up with one hell of a headache, and no one around to explain jack. I searched the whole building but couldn't find a soul in sight. Finally I borrowed some scrubs from a locker 'cause I couldn't find my clothes. I just decided to leave after a while. Walked right outside the front doors. I would've gotten in my car and driven away, but there weren't any cars either, including mine."

"I caught sight of a house across the street, a one-story ranch with a window lit up. I thought I saw some movement inside so I headed over. But when I knocked on the door, no one answered. I turned to walk away, but then a girl screamed from inside. I busted down the door and ran inside. The rest is history." He shrugged as if it didn't matter anymore.

"Who was screaming?" I asked sinking down into an armchair.

"That lunatic girl Jane." He answered just as I thought he would. I wasn't the first person Jane had lured in with her shrill screams. Finally I had found a common link. Maybe two. Jane was a link between Sam and me, and a clinic could be a link between Sam and David. And if John worked at that clinic as a doctor, he could have even more answers.

"Oh, hello, David. Who's your friend?" A delicate woman with graying black hair interrupted my thoughts. She had wrinkles at the corners of her eyes and mouth indicating that the toothy grin that she gave us was a common occurrence.

"Hey, Leslie!" David ran over and hugged Leslie. He picked her up, and she laughed halfheartedly protesting for her release. After another few protests, David set her down on her feet and began another set of introductions.

"Leslie, this is Ally. Sorry we didn't come to visit earlier, but you know how it is with new guests." He shot her an apologetic glance. "Ally, this is Leslie. She bakes the best cookies ever."

"Speaking of cookies," Leslie began, walking back into the kitchen, causing David to follow her like a dog on the hunt.

"You seem like a smart kid." Sam kept his voice low and turned up the television. He checked behind his shoulder before continuing. "Come back tonight at around eleven. Don't bring David."

I suppressed the urge to ask him why as I heard the cabinet in the kitchen close with a final thud. David walked back into the front room wiping his hands with a dish towel. Leslie followed behind.

"You've got quite a young man here." Leslie patted David on the back wearing the expression of a proud mother. "Helps out whenever he can," she continued.

I smiled awkwardly, unsure of the correct response.

"Anyways," she continued apparently unaware of my hesitation, "I put together a plate of sweets for the two of you." She held out the plate.

"Thank you." I held out my hands for the plate, still feeling out of place.

"My pleasure," she responded, taking me up in a hug. I hugged her in return, trying to back away after a moment. Still she held me, giving me no choice but to stand there awkwardly or initiate my hug once again. After hugging her back for the second time, she finally released me.

"See you later." I said my farewell mostly to Sam, knowing that I would be back.

"Bye, guys," David said as he gathered Leslie up into another hug and gave Sam a friendly shake.

They closed the door behind us, and I felt that I had succeeded in obtaining more questions than answers. I didn't think that I could wait until later to find out the news that Sam had for my ears alone.

David and I walked back toward the guest room quietly. I longed to go into David's room and fall asleep in his arms, but I forced myself to keep that distance. Once again we placed ourselves in separate bunk beds. As always, he took the bed closest to the door, and I went for the one in the middle. Our sleeping arrangement usually put me at ease, but I dreaded trying to sneak past him in the middle of the night.

Ally

Once I heard David's soft snores, I slid out of bed and tiptoed toward the door slower than a turtle. I opened the door an inch at a time, flinching each time it let out a squeak. I finally opened the door large enough to squeeze myself sideways through the space I had made. I left the door open so that I wouldn't have to go through all that once I came back and made my way down the hall with as much stealth as I could muster.

The hallway lights were still on which made it easier to avoid the walls and slip sideways to keep the light from falling on my head. Once I made it to the hallway that branched off to the left, I made my way down toward Sam's room. I kept an eye on the doorways, still expecting Jane to jump out of nowhere to *help* me.

My worries were eased as I finally reached the door at the end of the hallway and knocked lightly three times. I waited for five minutes, starting to doubt whether or not Sam was awake. I had made up my mind to leave when the door opened an inch revealing a sliver of light.

"Who's there?" Sam asked. He kept his voice low so I didn't feel as ridiculous creeping around the house like a burglar.

"It's Ally," I replied softly, still checking behind me to make sure that no one was there.

He opened the door slowly and also took a quick glance at the hallway. He motioned for me to come in with his hand and quickly closed the door once I was inside. I felt my heart thudding in my chest, and I stood there awkwardly, unsure of my next words. Luckily, Sam didn't keep me waiting long.

"I suppose we better get down to business. Go ahead and make yourself comfortable." He hit the couch and then sat in the chair across from it that he had been sitting in earlier. "I have to admit that I may have bent the truth a bit when you came here earlier. I just don't have the heart to lie anymore." He watched me carefully.

"Lie about what?" I asked numbly. I noticed that he had placed himself between me and the door.

"About why we're here of course," he answered simply. "Well actually, I don't know why everyone is here. I only know about the circumstances of a few of us. And even those explanations are incomplete. All I can do is to offer you a little bit of insight."

"I've already gotten some insight from the guy in the lab coat, if that was even real." I cut in, not wanting to hear another triumphant explanation about the advances in research putting unsuspecting people into a crazy world that only existed in their minds.

"When did this happen?" he asked. It was good to see that I could surprise someone for a change instead of being the one with my mouth hanging open.

"Today, before I came to see you. He told me all about the research that they're doing." I felt smug, believing that I knew everything and didn't need Sam to reveal anything.

"Well, I entered this program voluntarily, and it wasn't for research," he shot back, putting me in my place. "I was diagnosed with lung cancer about three years ago. My doctor offered me something that I guess you could call a new nontreatment."

"That sounds like research to me," I interrupted despite my better judgment.

"Sorry," I apologized as Sam glared at me.

"It's not research. It's a form of hospice." He revealed the new information calmly. I had expected him to yell at me for interrupting.

Suddenly, I was wishing he would have yelled instead.

"The doctor offered me an opportunity to go into a medically-induced coma in which I could live out the rest of my life without experiencing the pain that the cancer would cause. I should've looked at the fine print though. I had no idea that I would be living in a place like this." He fell silent, staring into space.

"We're all in comas right now, and it's definitely not for hospice." I insisted. I didn't care that Sam had been told it was end-of-life care. I definitely hadn't been in a hospital dying.

"Perhaps it isn't," he agreed. "I'm beginning to see that now. That's why I wanted to speak with you."

He paused and took another cursory glance toward me.

"You should know that John was my doctor. Also, there were six girls before you," Sam revealed, finally giving me the shock that I had been expecting since walking in the door.

I didn't have anything to say in response. I sat there in silence, unable to accept that new piece of information but at the same time feeling stupid for not uncovering it sooner.

"John's the insider that creep was talking about," I said more to myself than to Sam.

"So you knew this was just in our minds the whole time?" I asked feeling angry that it seemed like people I had come to trust knew the truth—or at least a version of the truth.

"Who else knows?" I demanded.

"Leslie, my wife, signed up for the program despite my complaints. That was when I started to have second thoughts about the true purpose of the program. You see, Leslie was completely healthy. I don't know if anyone else knows about our situation other than Leslie and John. I've always had my suspicions about Jane, but I couldn't prove it."

"So David doesn't know?" I asked hopefully. I didn't want to hear that David had been lying to me the whole time as well.

"I'm not sure about anyone in this house, that's why I asked you to come here alone." He reminded me in a tone that made me feel stupid. "There's a strict 'see no evil, hear no evil, speak no evil' policy here that makes it impossible to discover anyone's true motives."

"You could've wanted to speak with me alone because he didn't want you to tell me the truth," I pointed out, spiraling into doubt.

"I suppose you're right," he conceded.

I sat there for a moment, trying to decide my next move. I could have confronted John, but I wasn't sure anymore if he was someone that I could trust. I could have told David the truth, but he might have been involved as well.

"What happened to the other girls?" I asked.

The silence I received in response was deafening.

"What happened to them?" I repeated after a moment.

"I'm not quite sure," Sam responded.

"But they all disappeared," he added, giving me the chills.

"I have to get going."

I stood up, trying not to seem too eager to leave. I didn't want Sam to hold me back just because he wanted to stay in a coma while he died.

"I would go to Michelle first. She's the most understanding," he offered. Apparently, I was more transparent than I thought.

I nodded and walked out the door, trying to keep myself from breaking into a run in my eagerness, but when I closed the door, I felt lost and unsure of my next move. On top of the fact that everyone was probably sleeping right then, I felt like confronting anyone else before David would be a betrayal, and whether or not he had betrayed me was yet to be determined.

I walked down the hallway, turning left toward the kitchen in search for something to eat. I ran through my options in my head, trying to decide which one would be best. I was so focused on my thoughts that I hadn't even registered the argument coming from the kitchen—an argument that would throw me for a loop for the second time that night.

Ally

I stood outside the kitchen door listening to Michelle and Eric arguing. At first, I had debated whether or not I should turn around and go back to my room, but before I could make a decision, I heard Michelle bring up the subject of Jane.

I felt like I needed to know whatever the couple was talking about. Maybe I was being rude eavesdropping, but as I stood there, my conscience stopped nagging at me and my anger began to rise.

"We're having another meeting tomorrow," Michelle spoke pleadingly.

"That's not good enough!" Eric yelled, causing me to shrink back against the wall as I imagined Michelle doing the same.

"What else would you have me do?" she asked, still pleading.

"Bring an end to this nonsense. Why should we all be involved in helping a girl that takes pleasure in our pain on a daily basis?" He lowered his tone but still sounded just as threatening, if not more.

"This is my job, Eric," Michelle responded flatly.

"Well, it's a crappy job. Don't you dare tell me that you enjoy it," Eric argued.

"But imagine the amount of good we can accomplish." She was defending herself, trying to get Eric to see her point of view and sounding just like all the other white coats.

"You don't need Jane to accomplish your goals, and you need consenting subjects." I could hear Eric's voice going softer, more understanding. "We've already learned so many dangers and have yet to learn anything helpful," he sighed.

I sat down on the floor, letting the breath I had been holding out in a rush. Michelle was definitely involved in the whole mess. From what I had heard, I assumed that Eric had either been another unwilling or uninformed subject that had discovered the truth.

"We'll have another meeting. Jane can change," Michelle insisted.

My heart pounded in my chest as if it was about to jump out of my body to get as far away as possible. I stood up, feeling light-headed as the blood that had been so forcefully coursing through my body rushed to my head. I forced my feet to move themselves toward the kitchen even though every cell in my body screamed to run.

I put my hand on the door, summoning the courage to turn the handle and confront the people that I had once thought of as friends, and suddenly thought of as potential enemies.

As it turned out, I didn't have to work up the nerve. David did it for me.

"Ally! You scared the crap out of me," he shook his head at me, walking toward the kitchen from down the hall.

"Sorry I couldn't sleep," I lied. There was no way that Michelle and Eric hadn't heard David's reprimand.

"Me neither," he replied coolly, coming up next to me and wrapping his arm around my shoulder. "You know what that means," he smiled and waited for my guess.

"Cold medicine?" I guessed, shrugging my shoulders.

"Something way better," he goaded, waiting for me to guess again.

"Milk and cookies," he supplied when I didn't take another stab at guessing.

"Come on," he exclaimed, grabbing my hand and dragging me into the kitchen.

As I had expected, we walked in on Michelle and Eric. They were sitting across from each other, quietly eating cookies.

"Hey, guys," David greeted them, completely ignorant of everything.

"Hey," they grunted simultaneously, glancing up at David briefly.

Michelle glanced nervously at me, and I stared back, defiantly trying to convey both my new knowledge and my opinion without David noticing. Michelle's eyes quickly darted back to her hands on the table.

"Geeze, who died?" David asked, jokingly.

"They're probably just anxious about the meeting tomorrow." I snorted. I didn't want those two to get comfortable again as David lightened the mood.

"Meeting?" David asked, all trace of light-heartedness gone.

"Yes, David, there's a meeting tomorrow at eight o'clock. We're going to discuss Jane's actions and decide on a punishment," Michelle replied, begging me with her eyes to remain quiet.

"It's about time," David snorted, plowing into the pile of cookies.

"I'm not hungry," I cut in bluntly, refusing to participate in the charade.

"We better get some sleep." I stared pointedly at Michelle and walked out of the room.

"Wait up," David called from behind me.

"What is up with you?" he asked, studying me.

"I'm just tired," I lied again, staring at the floor.

"All right," David started, sounding unconvinced but deciding not to challenge me.

"Okay," I agreed, walking toward the room again and feeling the guilt bubbling up as I considered the fact that I was hiding the truth from David.

"Why didn't you tell me about the other girls?" I asked David. He had to have met them.

David stopped in his tracks, staring at me intensely. He opened his mouth a few times as if he wanted to speak, but forgot what he was going to say each time he began.

I crossed my arms, waiting for an answer. I had lived there and followed along blindly for too long.

"There were seven other girls. Each of them disappeared within a few weeks," he answered quietly.

"What happened to them?" I asked shortly. "I thought no one could leave," I pointed out accusingly.

"They didn't leave. They just disappeared," he shook his head and stared at the wall. "They each came back when they died. One day we woke up, and they were just gone."

"You didn't think to tell me this before?" I demanded.

"I didn't know how," he defended himself, throwing his hands up in the air.

"You knew I was looking for answers!" I yelled. I tried to keep my voice and temper down but I was beginning to realize that no one was telling me the truth.

"I was trying to protect you."

"That's not good enough." I walked into the guest room and sat down on my bed.

"I'm sorry." David sat down next to me, waiting for a response.

"Can I trust you?" I asked, feeling utterly alone.

"Yes," he promised, taking my hand in his. "I will always protect you," he swore, bringing my hand to his lips again. I didn't laugh.

Instead, I leaned forward kissing David for the first time since my near-death experience, for the first time since he had declared his love for me. Although I was incredibly scared and still unsure of whom I could trust, I needed to put my faith in someone. He put his hand to my face and deepened the kiss. I pulled away after a few moments and searched his face hoping to see that the words he spoke matched his expression. He looked as lost as I did, but his face was set with a certain determination. There and then, I chose to put my faith in David.

David

I woke up in the morning, finding Ally's bed empty again. I ate breakfast quickly, eager to walk around the house and *accidentally* run into Ally. I checked the gym, figuring that she liked to run when she was stressed. After finding the gym empty, I walked down the hall to Sam's room, thinking that maybe Ally had more questions. I decided that if I didn't find Ally there, I would look for John next, and then Michelle and Eric to see if she was questioning them.

"Hey, David," Michelle stopped me halfway down the hallway.

"Hey, have you seen Ally?" I asked

"Yeah, she's in the kitchen," she answered.

"She was acting pretty weird last night," I fished for information.

"You have no idea," Michelle replied vaguely. "Just come with me," she insisted in response to my questioning look.

We walked to the kitchen in silence. Michelle walked ahead of me, dissuading any form of conversation.

"John just . . . he just disappeared right in front of us!" Ally ran up to us wide-eyed and out of breath.

"It's okay, this is a good thing," Michelle cut in soothingly.

"What do you mean this is a good thing?" I asked turning on her.

"What's going on?" I demanded.

"We can leave," she answered simply.

"Leave?" I asked stupidly.

"Well actually, we can't leave, not like Ally can, but we're going to be taken out." Michelle offered, still leaving out information.

Ally walked over to Sam, grabbing his hand and squeezing it. Leslie did the same on Sam's other side.

I walked away, needing privacy as I thought about what the new development meant to everyone. Guilt sprung up as I walked down the hallway, a new leak springing with each one I plugged. What would become of Jane and Ally?

Ally

"John was taken out to oversee the process," Michelle continued after David left, still managing to bring up more questions than answers.

"Why now? What process?" Leslie asked, shooting Sam worried glances every now and then.

"The whole point behind this situation we're in now was to wake Jane up from her coma. She was involved in a car accident when she was younger, and her parents funded this area of research to try to help her." Michelle confessed sadly.

"So what happens to Sam?" Leslie asked. "This is hospice for him!" she yelled.

"If I know the men that make up this team, there's a pretty good chance that you are perfectly healthy," Michelle offered.

"Figures" was all Sam had to say before both he and Leslie disappeared.

"How can you work for them?" I asked, staring at the empty space.

"I work for every person that was in this house. It may seem like I go along with everything, but I promise you that's not the case." Michelle touched my shoulder.

I glanced back at her wondering whether or not she would also disappear at the same time as Eric. I clasped my hands, fighting the urge to go in search of David. For all I knew, he was already gone too. Would we continue to be lab rats after Jane was restored to full health? We'd fulfilled our purpose, and it wasn't like they could just let us go after making us their unwilling captives. Michelle and John would be safe since they worked for the nameless research division. Eric would probably squeak by too, but I couldn't see a happy ending in store for Sam and Leslie, and I definitely could not see things going well for me.

"There's one more thing I need to tell you," Michelle cut in on my thoughts, taking her hand back when I glanced at it.

"Of course there is," I sighed dramatically, even adding an eye roll that would make Jane proud.

"Ally, Jane's brain was damaged in the car accident," Michelle said, confirming my suspicions that the girl was mentally unstable.

"So they figured out a way to fix her?" I asked lamely, not understanding how that had anything to do with me.

"No, they couldn't find a way to reverse the damage, and unfortunately Jane couldn't go back to her body in that state." Michelle talked to me like a doctor who had a dying family member of mine in the other room.

"So is she dead?" I asked, picturing how pissed off her parents would be after investing a butt ton of money, only to find out that their daughter was dead. It wasn't like they could sue though after investing money in illegal experimentation.

"No," Michelle answered slowly, stalling for time. I could hear the implied but, or however.

"Could you please just spit it out," I snapped, sounding harsher than I had intended, but getting the job done.

"Whether they succeeded or failed in their attempt to get Jane back into a body, your body," she corrected, "there's a very good chance that you will not be able to wake up," she said in a rush, trying to keep eye contact but continuously averting her glance to the floor.

"What?" I asked incredulously.

"They cross-mapped your brain wave pattern onto Jane's, and any attempt they make to put Jane's consciousness into your body could alter your brain so much that it doesn't recognize your consciousness."

"Huh?" I started laughing then, delirium bubbling up inside of me. "So you're on *everyone's* side, huh?" I asked sarcastically.

"Please, Ally, you have to try to leave before it's too late," she begged, shaking my shoulders.

"What will happen to me?" I asked seriously, the laughter fading just as quickly as it had come.

"This world was created by Jane but altered by researchers," Michelle started. "With her gone, I suppose you would continue to live in it, possibly changing your surroundings based on your thoughts and emotions. They wouldn't be able to get to you anymore, but believe me, Ally, this is not the life you want," she insisted.

I ran out of the room without a second thought, making a mad dash for the stairs, only stopping when I reached the front door. I reached for the doorknob, but doubt crept in. What if I failed? I couldn't end everything with David like that. I ran back up the stairs, hoping that he hadn't disappeared yet.

I didn't want to pass up the opportunity to get one last glimpse at David, to tell him how I felt and could come to feel if we had more time, and to warn him about the mess he would wake up in. I pictured Jane kissing David with my body and shuddered.

Usually, I felt nervous when confessing feelings. Maybe the fact that I might never see him again made the possibility of rejection less threatening. Or maybe the life-threatening situation was pushing me to say things that I would never say or things that I hadn't completely thought out. Maybe it the possibility of dying to make me live.

David

I continued to pace up and down the hallway but, as it has a habit of doing, guilt continued to nag at me until I gave in and circled back toward the kitchen. I ran into Ally before I could get back to the meeting.

"They're all gone!" Ally sobbed, running up to me and throwing her arms around my waist.

"It's okay," I reassured her, sounding like Michelle.

"Last night, I went back to Sam's, and he told me that he knew why he was here, except he didn't know. They lied to him."

She shook her head sadly but didn't let me ask about Sam as she continued to babble. "Then I heard Michelle and Eric arguing in the kitchen. Michelle's in on this, David," she added hesitantly. "This, this change is good for you, but it's different for me." She stopped, hugging me close.

"How so?" I asked carefully.

"I can't leave!" she cried, pushing me away.

"Ally." I reached for her hand, but she stepped back, out of reach. "What do you mean you can't leave?" I asked, letting my hand fall like a wounded soldier.

"Maybe you should've just let me die," she hiccupped, continuing to cry. "But then you and everyone else wouldn't be able to leave now. Maybe this is a good thing. It's not like I was doing anything special with my life."

"That's ridiculous," I said, trying to bring her back. I reached out to her again, but again she resisted.

"You're not listening to me, David!" she yelled, coming face-to-face with me.

"You're not making any sense," I screamed, refusing to watch her accept the turn of events.

"Nothing is as it seems," she warned.

"I'm saying good-bye," she added with finality as I began to feel dizzy, and the ground fell away from beneath my feet.

"I love you," her voice echoed in the darkness.

"Just go!" I yelled, knowing that if anyone could get out of that house by themselves, it was Ally. She was brave and beautiful in a way that I hadn't seen for years. I just couldn't get the words out of my mouth before I disappeared into space.

Ally

I sat on the floor next to the front door staring at the wooden frame. I had run through the door frame again and again with no results. I had paced around the room and even up and down the stairs. I was desperate for a solution, for a way to get out, but I sat on the floor feeling sorry for myself. I couldn't move myself to get up. The tears had slipped out before I could stop them, pouring down my face in a torrent. I sat there quietly trying to keep the sobs securely stifled.

Finally, the grain of the wood took away all thought, pulling me into its pattern, allowing my eyes to wander over the lines and knots. At some point, I gave in to my drowsiness and fell into a restless sleep, not even remembering making the conscious decision to lie down.

I dreamed of hospital beds and doctors yet again. Again, I was in a bed. The doctors were completely ignoring me as they continued to run in and out of the room. Jane appeared above me, a triumphant look on her face, and snapped the wrist restraints on me with a harsh click. When she started to laugh, I expected her to walk away and leave me stranded, maybe taunting me first.

Instead, she climbed onto the cot and leaned over me, her face close to mine.

"Free at last!" she declared gleefully.

"I don't do girl-on-girl," I shot back, trying to sink into the cot as far as I could.

"I don't know what everyone will do without your clever comebacks," she said as her body disappeared, actually sinking into me. At first emotions that I rarely experienced flooded my body. I felt enraged, bitter, and then envious which was quickly covered up by cold calculative planning. I couldn't think straight, my thoughts pushed to the back of my mind. I felt like I was still trapped in the house, staring at the front door.

Then, my mind began to clear, and I started to think I'd imagined everything when Jane began to get up from the bed, passing through me again. She turned around and winked at me, but she wasn't Jane anymore. She had my face!

"Thanks so much." Jane laughed with my voice too. Her laugh still had the same cold tone though. "I'm thinking this should make David take me back."

I fought against my restraints, tipping over the bed and falling to the floor, knocking over a bunch of equipment as I went. A glass jar smashed against the wall, and the liquid within it doused an electrical plug, causing a small flame to spark into life from the short circuit.

The flames licked at my arm, and a shrill scream rang out, causing everyone to stop their hectic scrambling and finally turn their attention to us. The scream surprised even me, but maybe I was just in shock. I looked over at Jane, about to yell at her to get a fire extinguisher because I couldn't really stop, drop, and roll since I was strapped to a bed that was probably about to catch on fire any second.

The screaming continued, and I glanced up at Jane. I realized that she was actually the one screaming as her arm began to blister, even though the only flame in sight was quickly spreading up my arm.

My restraints snapped open, and I sat up, trying to roll over my arm to put the fire out, wondering what kind of training the room full of doctors could possibly have if they just stood there staring stupidly throughout the whole event.

I woke up rolling away from the sun in the main room of the house. There was no fire, but my sleeve was charred and arm was blistered in the same way I had seen in my dream. Whether or not my dream was reality, fiction, or a mixture of both, I was sick of it.

The constant concern that I was insane surfaced with greater force. At least before then, there were other people apparently going through the same crisis, but all of a sudden I was alone, having odd dreams about body theft. In addition, injuries in my dreams were appearing when I woke up.

I tried to reason with myself. Obviously, I was under a lot of stress because everyone had disappeared.

Plus, the part of my dream about burning my arm was probably real, physical pain from rolling into the sun. Then again, I wasn't actually corporeal. My body back in the lab was the real thing. Still, I circled back around, remembering the dream I had when Jane stabbed me—the dream where doctors back in the lab were trying to stop the bleeding and sew me up.

Whatever had just happened, my arm continued to nag at me, and I decided that a first aid kit would do me much more good than falling asleep next to a source of fire again. I walked up the stairs toward the bathroom, trying to analyze my dream.

Jane stealing my identity could have meant many things. It could've been my way of dealing with my inability to get back into my body. Maybe it was my mind making up an excuse for why I couldn't get back. Or maybe, just as my arm burning had been quite literal, Jane had actually taken over my body. I shivered, imagining all the damage she would do.

Thinking about Jane stealing my body and using it for her own purposes made me sick. There was no way in hell that Jane or any scientist could lock me out of my own body. I opened the first aid kit from the bathroom medicine cabinet and searched for some type of bandage and began to laugh.

Before I had walked in there, trying to save Jane of all people, I had been afraid of Freddy Krueger. But suddenly I found myself waking up with injuries that I attained while in my dream.

I wrapped the gauze over my arm, cutting off the circulation when my thoughts got too out of control. I sighed, unwrapping the gauze and then rewrapping it.

"Get a hold of yourself," I muttered, staring myself down in the mirror. Then shook my head, realizing that controlling myself yet again was probably a mistake. If Jane had my body who knew what she was doing with it.

I ran down the hallway, taking the stairs two at a time as I reached them. Determination to walk out the front door and never come back filled my veins with fire as my heart pounded in anticipation. I paused when I got to the front door. My hands were shaking as I placed my right hand on the door and left hand on the doorknob. I took a deep breath and prepared to fight through the haze to get my body back.

Sure, my dream could have been just a dream, but they seemed to have a knack for coming true. I opened the door and stepped outside, imagining the white room with doctors in lab coats. I saw everyone hooked up to heart monitors and brain monitors, and God knew what else.

At first, I could almost feel myself floating back into my body just like the first time. But that came to an abrupt halt as I hit a brick wall. I stopped, putting my hand out in front of me, trying to push my way through, even punching and kicking when that didn't work.

Three other walls and a ceiling began to close in on me, and I started hyperventilating, drowning in air instead of water.

"Stop!" I yelled, putting my hands out.

"You can't do this to me." I sobbed before I could stop myself. I shook my head. Falling apart wouldn't get me back to my body.

"You cannot do this to me," I yelled with more conviction, causing the wall in front of me to crack and release tiny clouds of dust and pebbles.

"You cannot use me!" I shouted at the wall, pushing it again with my hands and imagining I was pushing Jane. I thought of ripping her to shreds. The wall was cracking but not nearly enough. No matter how hard I fought, Jane had the upper hand.

Sure, I could argue that I was good, and Jane was evil but it wasn't that simple. It wasn't just black and white, and Jane could convince herself that she wasn't doing anything wrong if she wanted to. She could convince herself that she was justified, taking what was rightfully hers.

The wall began to seal up again, my doubt providing Jane with an advantage. My body may have been home territory, but right then, it was Jane's. My shoulders slumped when I realized my approach wasn't going to work. I thought about channeling any possible catty remark that I could think of toward Jane, but I couldn't see that working either. I wasn't going to lie to myself and say that I was better than that because I really wasn't. Only, my remarks would most likely entertain Jane.

Instead, I thought about myself and no one else. I thought about my motive of waking up and keeping Jane, in my body, away from David. I thought of her tricking David into sleeping with my body. No one was going to cash in my V card, but me.

I thought about myself as whole and pure, and then pictured her as torn and frayed. I remembered each evil action that she had committed. I remembered when she stabbed me and pictured the knife that had sliced through my stomach piercing her as well. I recalled the joy she had while watching others suffer and imagined pieces of her flaking off like dead skin with each act. Whether or not she was evil, she had made it her soul purpose to help herself at the expense of others so really, without anyone around her she was nothing.

The wall became cloudy and smoky, almost like a frayed sheet. I was surprised by how much it resembled the image I had of Jane falling apart. I walked through the cloud, coughing like I did every time I came into contact with cigarette smoke. I laughed, thinking of Jane as second-hand smoke—dangerous and unwanted by everyone in the room.

I woke up with David staring at me. He looked furious and as close to violence as I had ever seen him.

David

Hearing Ally's declaration of love had made my heart pound. The falling sensation was a completely separate sensation however. It felt exactly like when I had attempted to leave the house, but in the end I woke up in an uncomfortable, plastic coated chair.

"What are you doing?" John's voice spoke above me. He spoke to the balding man in the white lab coat with a strange familiarity that implied the two men knew each other. I tried to sit up but was held down tightly by restraints around my ankles and wrists.

"We figured that if Ally could wake up, we could map those brain waves into Jane's brain waves, forcing her to wake up. You see, it was basically the reverse of mapping Jane's brain waves into everyone else, forcing them into her world.

"And as you should've anticipated, your plan didn't work." John spoke loudly and I could tell that his anger was beginning to simmer. Only a small amount of provocation would cause his emotion to boil over. "Jane's mind is damaged. It's a miracle that the world she created in the first place wasn't completely illogical."

"Although Jane didn't wake up in her body, she is now conscious to this world. Everyone here, even Jane's parents—although still new to the idea—consider the results of our endeavor a success."

"Undo this Andrew. Put her back to sleep." John ordered.

"Sorry, but her parents agree that while Jane's body and mind have significant damage from the car accident, Ally's body is a much better option. I hate to tell you that we also have our supervisor's approval. You have absolutely no say," the stranger gloated.

"There have been much worse consequences to the study than this," he reminded everyone in the room.

"This is what we wanted!" he exclaimed.

"We're all here, but Ally isn't? Where's Ally then? Still in the house?" I kept rattling off questions, but the men around me looked like they either didn't care to answer or didn't have an answer. Some looked pleased, some looked upset, but most just looked confused.

"Hey, D." A face entered my vision and as my eyes focused I recognized Ally's pear-shaped face.

"Ally! Thank God you're okay. These people here have been saying you won't wake up. I told you it would be okay," I sighed in relief.

"Why are you calling me D?" I questioned.

"Oh, I'm hurt. I thought that you would remember my little pet name for you. I guess I can't blame you though, I'm not exactly myself." She cracked up then, glancing into a little handheld mirror.

"I don't know what excuse for a facial cream this girl has been using." She clicked her tongue and placed the mirror back into her pocket.

"What are you talking about?" I didn't understand anything that was happening around me. I didn't even know what questions to ask anymore.

"Try to keep up D. As you know I, Jane, was in a coma, but luckily my parents had the cash to wake me up, granted in a slightly less superior body."

"That's enough, Jane," an anonymous guy in a lab coat chided.

"Fine. Just one more thing though." She faced toward me, looking pleased and taking a deep breath. "Your precious little Ally is either stuck in that house or gone to the world. Who knows how it works. I'm sure all the brainiacs in here can't even give you a straight answer as to where your little pet is right now. But you should be relieved you don't have to babysit anymore. And now you're free to . . ." She trailed off at the end, tilting to the side and almost collapsing completely before my father caught her.

"Get me out of this chair right now!" I yelled at everyone in the room, fighting against the restraints.

"Ally? Or Jane? Hello? Are you okay?" John shook Ally. Or I guess more accurately he was shaking Ally's body. She began to thrash out, fighting for air and fighting John at the same time. She fell silent for a moment and then slowly regained consciousness, a burn forming on her arm.

"W-what happened?" she asked, sounding shaken. Good, if Jane was going to steal my kind-of girlfriend's body, then I hoped she suffered.

"Get some cream for this burn," John ordered.

"Jane?" he asked, watching her carefully.

"Who else would it be?" she snapped, wincing as she yanked her arm away.

"Oh, I don't know, maybe the girl that the body actually belongs to," I snarled.

"You better be nice," she chided. "After all, you're not in much of a position to defend yourself." She began to saunter over to me, moving her hips from side to side in an exaggerated motion.

"Jane, we have some issues to discuss," John interrupted, touching her shoulder with his hand.

"Oh, come on," she whined, "it can't be that important." She turned toward John, sticking out her lower lip in a pout.

"It is that important Andrew cut in, returning with a first aid kit. "Not here though," he added, glancing at me.

"Fine," she agreed following his gaze.

The three of them walked away, Andrew fussing over Jane's arm, Jane executing her exaggerated hip roll, and John glancing back at me with his best apology face. He was going to have to do a lot better than that if he ever wanted me to speak to him again.

I watched them discuss the mystery problem behind the glass window of an office connected to the lab. At first, Jane looked worried, but after a few more moments of comforting gestures and words from both John and Andrew, she looked pleased.

Unfortunately, the expression was planted on Ally's face, the emotions that played out torturing me. To see someone I cared for standing so close but know that Jane was the one pulling the strings shook me to my core. Nothing would ever be the same.

Finally they stopped talking, leaving the room and heading toward me again. Jane stalked toward me, but before she could say anything, she fell to the ground again. She stayed completely still. While she was unconscious, the doctors began to bandage her arm and check her vitals. The gloating doctor looked so worried that I imagined him dashing for the door, trying to reach the border before Jane's obviously well-off parents could get a hold of him.

I continued to fight against my restraints, completely forgotten.

"What happened?" Jane asked again, finally regaining consciousness.

"You passed out," John explained as he eyed her speculatively. He offered her his hand which she surprisingly accepted. Maybe the two of them were actually chummier than I had thought.

"Oh, so none of it was real?" she asked. Her comment confused me even more. Maybe even Jane's consciousness was seriously damaged in whatever accident she had been in.

"I'll never forgive you for this," I spat out. "I'll never forgive myself," I added.

Jane jumped and stared at me with wide eyes.

"Don't even pretend that you're the victim. You actually stole Ally's body! I will never forgive you, Jane." I spat at her, still struggling with the restraints.

Jane looked around the room, assessing all the men in white coats. "Well, if you ask me, I did do you a favor." She laughed, still eyeing her surroundings. "You've got a more experienced soul in the body that you crave so much." She trailed off at the end, her comment sounding more like a question than an actual statement.

"Just because we slept together doesn't mean you're an expert." I didn't care if the whole room of people heard me. I was getting really tired of her belief that she was so experienced.

"I really need to use the bathroom. Anyone care to show me the way?" She actually sounded hurt which should've caused me great joy, but I couldn't get used to saying hurtful things to Ally, even if she was possessed by the devil himself.

"Oh yeah, one more thing," she added, sounding her normal vindictive self yet again.

She bent over me and placed her lips next to my ear. I had the strange feeling she was going to kiss me, but instead she whispered into my ear.

"I know you think I'm Jane," she urged, sounding unsure and just as confused as I was. "But I swear to you that I really am Ally." She stood up, looking around her yet again and placing that snotty sneer back into place.

"Prove it," I said, not even bothering to lower my voice. It was probably just another intricate plan to hurt me.

"What's going on?" Andrew asked, interrupting our conversation. Jane, or maybe Ally, stiffened as she heard the man speak and bit her lip as she turned to face him.

"Just having a little fun. So where's the bathroom in this place?" she asked as she headed to the door.

"Down the hall to the right," John answered, waving off a security guard as he went to follow her. As soon as the girl who could be either Jane or Ally left the room, John finally released me from my restraints. I just shook my head and ran out the door, not caring about the protests that I left behind.

Ally

"Wait," David called as he ran down the hall after me. I stopped and glanced at his face trying to guess his intentions. David closed the distance between us and, cupping my face in his hands, gave me the sweetest kiss. A shock ran through me as the heat of his kiss coursed through my body. He ran his fingers through the hair at the nape of my neck exciting my nerves with electrical charges.

I stepped back abruptly as common sense took hold. He thought I was Jane just moments before. Maybe he had decided he wanted Jane after all, or maybe he just wanted my body. Ick. Either possibility was unbearable to handle.

"Ally?" he asked uncertainly.

"So now you believe me?" I questioned him, not daring to hope that he would happily declare that he was absolutely sure that I was, well, me.

"You bite your lip when you're nervous." He traced his finger along my lower lip, causing my body to react again.

"But Jane could know that. She could do it to fool you. You couldn't possibly be certain," I argued, slapping myself mentally for trying to convince David that I wasn't me.

"Jane would never bite her lip. First of all, she would probably make some lame statement that lip biting is unfashionable. But think about it. Have you ever seen her show any sign that she was scared? I just know, okay?"

"I don't know," I replied. "I can still feel her in here somewhere though," I confessed, tapping the side of my head as I fought to keep control of my fear. David took my hands and studied my face carefully.

"But you can't hear her thoughts, right?" His words sounded off somehow, almost like a dissonant chord struck on a piano.

"No, she's just like a pressure pushing down on my consciousness. It's like she's jammed in the back of my brain."

"That's great." He sounded relieved.

"Yeah," I lied, not at all relieved. Jane was still there, and David, although he may not have lied, was not completely honest with me either. "You wouldn't want me to hear all about the two of you having sex."

I kept my eyes down and voice low. But before David could comment, John entered the hallway.

"Hey, you two," John called. I tried to push all thoughts of Jane and David having sex out of my head because at that moment, I had to focus on being Jane.

That wasn't too hard though; Jane hated everyone, and at that moment, I definitely hated John. He was a traitor. He and his colleagues had put me in an awful situation, and they didn't give a damn that—to the best of their knowledge—I was still trapped inside Jane's house, or maybe even worse.

I gave John my best scowl and actually felt pretty confident that I could fool him. Unfortunately, I didn't have a game plan. Obviously, I had to fool everyone; otherwise I would be strapped right back into the plastic chair.

"You can stop pretending, Ally. I knew something was happening when you, or rather Jane, passed out. Then you confirmed my suspicions when you woke up and gave me your hand after I offered assistance. Jane would never let me touch her." He explained his reasoning quietly as he continuously glanced over his shoulder. "It was only a matter of time before you broke through," he added excitedly.

"Why was it only a matter of time? I could've been dead for all you knew. Are you going to tell everyone else?"

Although I was interested in John's foresight, the matter of my reoccupation of my body becoming common knowledge held a higher priority. I noticed David watching me, which made me aware that I had been unconsciously chewing my lip. I stubbornly stopped myself, hating that I was apparently so predictable.

"Is she in there with you?" John asked as if he hadn't heard me speak.

"Are you going to tell everyone?" I repeated, showing my stubborn streak.

"No." John rubbed the sleep from his eyes and let out a tired sigh. "The doctors here, including me, have committed too many wrongs in the past five years. It's time I set things right. Now, is Jane still with you?"

"Yes," I finally answered after examining John's face. "But like I told David, I can't hear her or anything. I just know she's there."

"Okay," he spoke quickly. "First, we need to get you out of here." And with that he grabbed my hand and began leading me toward the exit.

We walked down the hallway past doctors and nurses. All of them gave us a friendly hello, but my paranoia continued to build. Did everyone in the hospital know that we were involved in experimentation against our will?

I wanted to keep my head down and avoid attention, but then I thought that maybe trying to avoid attention would actually call attention to me.

When someone said hello, I would usually respond with a smile and a polite greeting. But then I remembered that Jane would do neither of those things, so instead I acted cold and distant, letting John speak while I stayed silent.

When we reached the exit, I was almost near hysteria. I never wondered how we managed to get out so easily.

David

"Hello, lover," Ally's voice seductively whispered into my ear. We had rented a hotel room and paid in cash so that the hospital couldn't find us. Falling asleep next to Ally again had felt right, and I had expected a quiet, uneventful night until she began kissing my neck, nipping at the side while slowly inching her hand closer to the crotch of my pants. Shivers ran up my back as I looked into Ally's eyes questioningly. I hadn't expected her to move this that fast. Just days ago, she had seemed terrified to think of having a romantic relationship with me. I looked over at the next bed only to find that John was no longer in it.

Reclaiming my attention, Ally examined my body with her fingertips with a furious, burning passion. None of her characteristic doubt lingered, and her vulnerable doe eyes were replaced with those of a predator. Ally rolled on top of me furiously kissing my neck, my face, my mouth. Her tongue invaded my mouth in earnest. I couldn't suppress the moan that slipped from my lips as the adrenaline coupled with desire coursed through my body and clouded my mind.

I began returning her kisses, and the passion built, a feeling so great and so torturous at the same time. When I finally felt that I couldn't hold back any longer, Ally pulled herself away from me and slid her shirt up and over her head, almost simultaneously heading for the buttons of my pajama bottoms.

I grabbed her hand, finally coming to my senses. We weren't ready no matter how good it felt. Besides, Ally had been flung into an emotional crisis over the new resident living inside her head with no say in the matter.

"What?" she asked, giving me a sly, sideways grin. "Don't tell me you don't want me, D." She laughed manically, and the chill that had felt so good before turned into a cold, numbing dread in the pit of my stomach.

"What did you just call me?" I demanded, pushing her off me. As soon as I managed to untangle myself from the mess of arms and legs, she jumped right back on top of me. I felt more like a wrestler being pinned against his will.

"What would Ally think if I told her that we've had sex? That while you were *courting* her we were still together?" she asked, knocking the breath out of me with both her body and her threat. "I bet you never even told her we kissed. Wouldn't it just blow her mind if she knew?" High-pitched cackling escaped as she threw her head back in a shrill note that couldn't belong to Ally's sweet face.

I threw what I understood to be Jane off me. She landed on the floor, knocking her head on the wall.

"Wow, I never thought you could abuse a girl like that. I'll really have to warn Ally about you. Maybe it would just be safer if I kept her away from you." She smiled her catlike grin.

"What do you mean?" I gasped stupidly.

"Well, I got control, didn't I? Maybe I could get used to this."

"She'll never let you!" I yelled, grabbing her shoulders. "You think you're all badass, but Ally is a hundred times stronger than you. You'll be gone soon enough!" My anger fled just as quickly as it had accumulated when the catty look transformed into fear.

"David? David, what are you doing?" She gasped, falling limply into my hands. "David, you're hurting me!" I quickly let go, and she fell back against the wall again, holding her hands tightly in a failed attempt to hide her tremors.

"Ally? Ally, I'm so sorry. Jane—she, well, she took over I guess you could say." I rushed to find words in a desperate attempt to explain myself before she jumped to the conclusion that I was a mad man trying to murder her in her sleep.

"Are you sure? I mean, you know I sleepwalk. And talk. I could've just been dreaming." She held her breath, hoping that I would ease her fears and concede that she could be right.

"I'm sorry, Ally. I'm sure."

Ally let out a deep strangled sound and buried her head in her hands as her shoulders slumped in defeat.

"Hey." I eased myself next to her. I could only think about trying to comfort her, but I was pathetically out of my league. What could I have said? Ally, I know how you feel? This happens to people all the time?

She had a psychopath locked inside her brain ready to take control at any moment.

I finally settled on "We'll go find John and figure this out." I pushed myself up against the wall and offered my hand to Ally. She looked up doubtfully but still placed her hand inside mine.

John

As soon as Ally and David fell asleep, I left the room, making my way to the room next door. I walked in on three men checking the sound system and took a glance toward the wall. What had looked like a mirror on the other side was actually a window. As the men finished their jobs, Ally began to wake up, and it soon became apparent that Jane was once again in control. The plan had succeeded, and the real work could begin.

CPSIA information can be obtained at www.ICGtesting.com
Printed in the USA
266821BV00002B/67/P